JUPITER

Sparks
Of
Betrayal

SPARKS OF BETRAYAL

21/03/23

SPARKS OF BETRAYAL

Part One (Meryl)

SPARKS OF BETRAYAL

JUPITER

I was born to solve crime. I've known since primary school. I was a problem solver, I'd make my friends create problems that I would spend hours solving. This moved onto crime solving kits I'd find in shops or my mother would make. She was the one to convince me to join the police cadets, I was adamant that they'd never let us do any real work but they did. They prepared us well. That's where I met Cristina. We did everything together from that point on, she was my partner in solving crime.

I had covered most things people learn at a university degree by the time I was thinking about my year eleven exams. After exams were over I carried on, even got to work in the police station helping them with small crimes around town. I dedicated my life to the police force. I worked day in and day out to get to the bottom

SPARKS OF BETRAYAL

of every single case handed to me and now what do I have to show for it? A few online articles and a couple of special mentions in crime documentaries. Memories, that's all those cases are now... ash and memories.

Chapter 1

I slammed into the front door in an attempt to escape. "It's locked... why is it locked?" I choked. I had only just come home, there was no way I had time to lock it. Besides, I never lock the door when I'm inside unless I'm going to bed and at three in the afternoon, I thought that highly unlikely. I ran towards the back door but soon realized that to be as futile as the front door as I hadn't even had time to unlock it since coming home. I was trapped. I could hear the roaring flames get stronger right above my head, the floor was about to give in. None of the windows opened wide enough for me to be able to climb through. I looked up at the ceiling, I could hear the wood melting... I ran to the furthest corner from where it would eventually collapse, right by the back door. *Perfect.* I thought. The only chance I had come from someone caring enough to phone for help, someone must have noticed by now.

As the seconds passed, the smoke began filling the air, I couldn't see anything, I laid on the ground wishing for someone to notice, hoping that just one person within the town cared enough to phone the fire brigade. I don't know what made me think they wouldn't, perhaps it was what had happened in past cases, perhaps I thought their jealousy had finally gotten the better of them and they would just watch the smoke rise with hope in their hearts that I was inside.

I was on the floor for what felt like forever, no one was coming. There were no sirens. No one cared. I had no choice but to prepare to die. I didn't know what I was supposed to do in terms of preparation, there wasn't really anything I could do, I couldn't move, or scream, or shout, or breathe. All I could really do was stare at the ceiling hoping they'd find the person who did this, it wasn't an accident, the timing of the blaze was too perfect for it to be an accident. Someone had waited for me to get home before setting something alight, someone had tried to kill me.

***

The next thing I remember, I was laying in the ambulance, I opened my eyes slowly, by now the entire house was engulphed in bright orange flames. Thick dark smoke bellowed from the roof. I couldn't feel anything, I grabbed the oxygen mask and tried to speak but nothing came out as I choked on the fumes.

"Don't speak, you're okay." the paramedic said softly as she readjusted the mask. "She's awake." she shouted.

"Well, there's something." I could hear the smile in his voice. "You had us worried there." I didn't recognize the voice, it was deep and rough like something I had heard before but couldn't quite figure out who it was.

"We need to go, now." the paramedics tone turned serious.

"Where is she going?"

"Golden Oaks General."

"Can I go with her?" the man's voice was angelic, deep and caring, crisp like winter air. I could imagine what he looked like based on how he sounded. His eyes were dark and so was his hair, almost jet black but not quite, his head would be long and his figure slender. When he smiles his bright teeth show.

SPARKS OF BETRAYAL

"Come on then." her voice sounded rushed which made me panic, what was wrong that made it so urgent. My whole body was shaking in fear.

Throughout my time in the ambulance, I drifted in and out of consciousness, every time I woke up, I could feel his hand in mine. I couldn't move my head down to see who he was so I was stuck with only my mental image of him. I could see the paramedic out of the corner of my eye I was hoping they'd swap places so I could see him but they never did.

"She's back again." His smile was still present in his voice. The sirens became louder, the man continued speaking but the words weren't reaching me. I stared at the ceiling terrified. I had no idea what was going on, and my legs were burning. I could feel the fire on my skin even though it wasn't there anymore, it was excruciating and there was no running from it.

I woke up again as we reached the hospital, to the rush of nurses around me as they wheeled me into the emergency room. By now the pain was getting stronger, and I began feeling every single inch of skin on my body.

By now I was really struggling to keep still but it was only making it worse. I could feel absolutely every movement,

JUPITER

every needle, every breath. I wasn't even sure my skin was still on my legs.

That was the last thing I remembered until I was in recovery.

Chapter 2

I stared out of the window; heavy rain beat the city. They sky was covered in dark blue rain clouds.

"Hey, you're awake! Hold on let me go get someone." the man said, he vanished before I had a chance to turn my head to look at him. The pain was somewhat bearable by now, I still couldn't feel a lot of my skin, but it wasn't so raw, and moving my head was so much easier because I wasn't strapped down to anything. I stared at the door waiting for the man to return.

A nurse walked in, "Hi Meryl, you were out for a while there."

"I–" I got distracted as the mystery man returned. I ignored his appearance for a moment.

"How long was I out? I was in the emergency room and then –"

"Three days." he said.

"Days!" I exclaimed choking on my gasp.

"You're lucky to be alive." the nurse said as she played with the wires behind me. "I've only ever seen one case as bad as that and they didn't make it passed the surgery doors."

"Steph!" the man gestured towards me.

"Sorry, all I'm saying is if Dylan hadn't dragged you out when he did, you'd have had no chance."

"Dylan?" I whispered.

"That's me." The man said. "I happened to be passing by and I just did what I knew. I'm a fireman." He reached out his hand to shake mine.

"Thank you." I said. "How did you get through the door?"

"Your friend opened it for me, he said you gave him a key in case of emergencies."

"Oh yeah, I forgot about that." I had never given anyone my house keys. All but one of my friends were dead, so I knew that was a complete lie.

The man smiled before walking away.

"He's dreamy isn't he." the nurse said.

"Hmm, not my type."

"Really? Detective Meryl Evans not into firemen?" The nurse asked.

"Detective Meryl Evans isn't into men." I giggled.

She laughed, "the doctor will be in soon to go through your injuries with you and they never found a cause of the fire so I'd imagine the police will be here soon too. If you need anything press this button, I'm number 23." She said, holding up a small box shaped device. She put it next to my hand and walked out.

I nodded and smiled before turning back to the window. I was alone again. The familiar mystery man wasn't familiar at all. He seems too suspicious to be trustworthy. Something was off about the key. Cristina would never have given the key to a stranger. Unless they were there and that was the only way to get in. I was angry and I had to stop looking for someone to blame, they were only trying to help.

JUPITER

The knock on the door startled me as the nurse came back. "Sorry, the police are here."

I smiled as Cristina walked through the door. Cristina and I had been friends since the beginning of police cadets.

"Detective Meryl Evans?" My stomach fluttered, "did you miss me?"

I've never stopped thinking about you. If I was given a blade of grass for every time, I thought about you I'd have my own field. A field with enough space to build our own house where we could grow old and care for each other. Every love song I've ever heard was all about you. Every love story I've ever read had your name written all over it. You are why none of my relationships ever worked out because you are whom the universe has chosen, you are the one I have chosen. You are the one my heart has chosen. Is what I wanted to say. I laughed at myself, I had never been any good at expressing love or whatever, I kept it all inside my head for no one to ever find out about.

"I have" I smiled.

"Can I sit?" She walked towards me slowly. I nodded. She sat. She was wearing the rose perfume I gave her for Christmas last year, I tried to hide my smile. We made eye contact which only rattled the butterflies in my stomach , I didn't know what to do at that moment. I couldn't move. My heart skipped a beat, she was too much for me, I didn't deserve to be in the presence of someone as perfect as her. I completely froze.

"Everything okay?" she asked.

I nodded, unable to speak. Her hair bounced as she looked back at me, her piercing blue eyes staring directly into mine.

"I uhhh –" I stumbled "What was it you wanted to talk about."

Her smile dropped, "Meryl... they never found a cause to the fire, and they say your front door was locked."

"So?"

"So, they've asked me to conduct an evaluation to determine whether you did it on purpose."

"What?" I scoffed.

"They wanted someone familiar to do it in hopes you would open up, but I can't lie to you."

"Do you think I would do that? Destroy everything, every single case I've ever solved and that single case I didn't solve. There was only one case in the whole thirty-seven years I didn't solve did you know that? Why would I destroy all of that?"

"I -" She stuttered.

"What?"

"You have been isolating yourself recently."

"So, you think –"

"No, the truth is I don't think that you would do it so that's why I thought I'd make sure you were okay."

"Clearly I'm fine so you can go." The last thing I wanted to do was turn Cristina away, but I couldn't bear her thinking I would do something like this to myself.

"Listen... I don't think you did it, but I don't think it was an accident either.

"Cristina." Dylan returned. "Can I borrow you for a moment."

"Give us a second."

"No Cristina, I need you now."

Cristina walked away, her rose scent went with her leaving me with nothing but the sterile scent of the hospital.

"The doctor is on his way now," Dylan said before closing the door.

A few minutes passed before Dr Will walked in.

"Meryl?"

"Yep." I said.

"How are you?" He tilted his head.

"Fine." My pain tolerance had always been abnormally high, but this was another level of pain. There was no way I was going to expose my vulnerability now though, I had to act as strong as possible because I knew the less, I gave away the faster I could get away from here.

"Has anyone been through the extent of your injuries with you?"

"No."

"Okay, do you want someone here with you or are you okay?"

"I'm fine."

"Okay so sixty percent of your body is covered in some kind of burn, the burns on your legs are third-degree. We performed skin grafts when you arrived."

"Surgery?"

"Where we remove the burnt skin and take skin from other parts of your body and move it to a different area of your body in this case your legs."

"When will I be out of here?" I asked.

"It usually takes about a month to heal and that's without complications."

"Complications?"

"Infection." He said, "we need to keep the burns wrapped to minimize the risk of infection, Steph's face will be one you never want to see again once it's over." he chuckled. "She'll be in most days to bring you food and clean your wounds."

I stared at the roof, the roof I'll be staring at for the next month. At least this gives me a chance to find somewhere else to stay.

"I'll leave you in peace now if you need anyone to talk to, we have hundreds of staff members here."

"Can people stop suggesting that I'm suicidal" I sighed.

Dr. Will tilted his head before leaving the room, and I was alone... again. This time it was nice, it was good to be alone for a while. I had been constantly interrupted by people, I was relieved they had finally stopped.

"A month" I sighed.

"A month of me can't be that bad right?" Steph stepped back into the room. I sighed as my loneliness was once again disturbed. "Sorry to disturb you again," she started, "you're a detective, right?"

"Retired now but, yeah."

"I thought you might like to see this." She held up a small burnt folder. I recognized it instantly, I had spent years trying to solve the murder of Ben Matthews. But how had Steph gotten hold of it? There was no way it survived that fire, there was simply no way anything could have survived it.

"Where did you get that!" I exclaimed.

"The firemen found it." She spoke.

"In the house...? there's no way."

"It was outside of the house... in the garden."

"What...? How did it get there?"

"I have no idea. Maybe you had taken it out to read?"

"Definitely not... I haven't touched that case in years..."

"I'll leave it here and you can figure it all out." She approached the bedside table where she placed the folder gently. "I'll be back tonight to bring you food but until then I won't let anyone disturb you."

I smiled, finally some undisturbed peace.

"But please, if you do need anything press the buttons." She smiled as she closed the door.

I looked over at the case. "A month to solve a murder," I whispered. I propped myself up gently every piece of my skin stinging as it was moved. I waited for it to settle before moving again. After a couple of minutes, I reached out for the case and pulled it towards me, it was rather light as I hadn't found much evidence at the time. I stared at the burnt cover. Someone must have taken it out of the house... someone must have saved it. It couldn't have been Dylan he would have arrived too late. No one else was there or surely, they'd have found me. The case was upstairs hidden in the closet... there's simply no way anyone would have known where to look. I looked at the wall as I tried to piece some kind of narrative together. None of it made sense.

SPARKS OF BETRAYAL

The Ben Matthews' case was my final case. A case I was given twenty years ago… a case I am yet to solve. I opened the folder and began rummaging through the evidence.

Chapter 3

The first thing I found was a documentation of the interviews, I held two to begin with, after a whole day of gathering evidence I was becoming frustrated as we weren't finding very much. Looking back I shouldn't have been so harsh but if there's one thing I've learnt it's that if you're too nice you'll get absolutely nowhere.

Hayley - 16:42 – Thursday 9th November 2000.

"Suspect A is Hayley Smith." I began the first interrogation. "Can you explain the day of 6th of November 2000?"

SPARKS OF BETRAYAL

"The rain was heavy; I remember the sound of it on the metal roof. My music wasn't loud enough to drown it out, so I used the sound as a prompt. My paints were already out from my last project, and I was trying to find an excuse to use my new canvas."

"What did you paint" I thought I'd ask just to act interested.

"Rain on the beach, I thought by combing something we all associate with summer and destroying the norm it would look quite effective." I wrote it exactly as she said it. It was somewhat fascinating how her brain worked but I had to ignore it and get to the bottom of this case.

"Do you paint for a living?"

"Yes, my paintings are my only income."

"Hayley, I have one final question, I appreciate your time" I smiled, "Did you have anything to do with the murder of Mr. Matthews?" Of course, I knew she wasn't going to just sit and confess.

"I would never do such a thing."

"Did you see him on the day of the fire?"

"Yes…" I could see her hands begin to shake; her tone began sounding suspicious too. That's when I thought… I've done it. I've got the murderer. But this was only the first suspect there were two others waiting, reciting their stories. I couldn't decide whether to keep asking questions, digging deeper into the relationship between herself and Mr. Matthews, digging deeper into the trauma that would have led her into this horrifying act, asking her more and more about the past and such until she snapped, or just letting her go back to her cell. The decision was near impossible, but I couldn't turn down the fun of interrogating two more suspects. Letting the first one snap would ruin the fun, I want my final case to be memorable… to go down in history… to change the world.

"Okay, thank you Hayley, that will be all for today."

The guard escorted her out of the room, something didn't feel right when she left the room. I had forgotten something.

"Actually Hayley, come back a moment please."

The guard sat her back down in front of me. Eye contact lasted about ten seconds before either of us said anything. In those ten seconds my mind filled with questions.

"What were you originally doing in that garage… you said you decided to paint after hearing the rain but what were you trying to do?" I asked with the hope that she would answer with 'concentrating' or along those lines, as she would be if she was planning to murder her best friend's boyfriend.

"I was going to read a book that had arrived that morning, but the rain was just too loud for me to keep track." She said, I believed it, but I still wasn't convinced of her innocence.

My next question was most likely one of the most important questions of the whole case... "Do you have proof of your whereabouts on this day, anyone who can confirm you were in fact painting in the garage? Anyone who can tell me whether you had planned to read that book? Any proof that you were even in that building?"

She looked down, there were few reasons a suspect would look down. Lies and being caught out. My guess was that she had no one to cover for her, everything she had said whether it's the truth or not couldn't count her out for the murder of Mr. Matthews and now she knew it.

"No" she muttered.

"I'm sorry can you say that again, clearer."

"No."

"Thank you." I find you get further being polite

"Do you have absolutely any proof at all that can confirm your innocence in the murder of Mr. Matthews?"

"I have the delivery time, I had to sign for it so I must have been at home to have it."

"Alright, do you know how you can send that to me? I need that in my case folder for it to have any value or for it to help your case at all."

"I'm not sure that's how it –"

"Shh, arguing with me won't help you at all." I had to stop her there I was beginning to get fed up with her voice, but I still needed something more, some more evidence. "Why did you agree to talk without a lawyer?" I knew the answer to this before asking but I needed to know if I was right.

"Because I'm telling the truth, I had nothing to do with his death so why would I need to pay someone to tell you that when I could just do it myself." I was right of course.

"But don't you think that makes you look more guilty?"

"How?"

"Well, you have no lawyer... maybe it's because no one believes you... maybe it's because you don't see a point in spending so much money if you're just going to end up going to prison for murder anyway. Maybe it's because you're hiding something from us, and you know that if a lawyer were to find it you would be sentenced almost immediately because no one wants to represent a murderer in court. People do it because they have to but no one wants to." Her body language shifted, I could see her becoming defensive, her eyes narrowed as if I had said something she didn't want anyone to know.

"That's ridiculous."

"What... that you have no lawyer or that you may be done for murder? That will be all, goodbye."

Had I just caught the murderer of my final case?

Chapter 4

The second interview I conducted was with the wife of the victim, this is the one with perhaps the most reason for murder. Living with someone is difficult, but promising to stay with them forever is harder. There had never been anything strange about Juno and Ben Matthews which made this interview all the more interesting for me. She was a suspect because she was close with him but honestly, I couldn't think of a motive.

Juno - 17:11 – Thursday 9th November 2000.

"Suspect B is Juno Matthews" I had decided this time that I would only state their name for the tape as all their information is in my folder, their addresses and ages weren't entirely relevant to this stage and so I kept them separate. "Where were you on the day of Mr. Matthew's murder?"

"I had gone out for the day, Ice skating with some friends. We left the house at 7 am for the 7:15 am train." She said with confidence, this was the initial thing that sent me into thinking she was guilty, I didn't ask her for times and yet she threw them at me. No one comes into an interrogation with that much confidence if they haven't learned what to say. Unless they were telling the truth, which was also a completely reasonable explanation.

"Can you confirm this?" I asked the man sitting on her left, this one seemed smart enough to get herself a lawyer.

He nodded.

"I can't voice record a nod, can I?" I chuckled pointing at the voice recorder. I thought a lawyer would at least be able to figure that out.

"Yes." He stated.

"Okay, I know Mr. Matthews was your husband... correct?"

"Yes, three years. Known him since primary school." She smiled.

"That's long enough to safely say you were fond of each other, which brings me to my next question. What was your reaction to Mr. Matthew's death? Where, how, when did you find out?" I needed as many details as possible, and I know these would be questions she would have prepared beforehand, especially if she was lying.

"I was on the train back from Cardiff, there were three of us sitting on a table seat, my phone rang but we were mid-game, so I didn't want to interrupt it. I silenced it and put it in my pocket, I continued playing until one of the girls had a message from an unknown number asking where I was, I didn't know who it was, so I ignored it again. They said it was urgent so in the end I gave in and phoned them back."

"When was this?"

"Between 21:30 and 22:00"

"What time did he die?"

"How is she supposed to know?" Her lawyer questioned.

"It's just a question." I scoffed, I had the right to ask questions, it was the whole reason we were there.

"What happened next?"

"They told me that the police had been round looking for me, so I asked why."

"Do we have proof of this phone call?"

"We do." Her lawyer placed a memory stick on the desk in front of me. I picked it up and placed it into the voice recorder.

"Are you going to play it now?" her voice shook. I never understood why they would present evidence and be nervous about hearing it, if it proved her innocence she could sit and smile, but she seemed nervous. I decided to listen to it privately first.

"Not just yet, I want to analyse it first. How did you react to them telling you the police were looking for you?"

"I was confused, I hadn't done anything to warrant them searching for me. That's when they told me they had found Ben."

"Did they tell you where or how or anything?" She really wasn't giving away enough details for me.

"She said he had been caught in a fire in town" This is where I had heard enough. Police wouldn't have told a stranger anything, either they knew what happened because they were there, or Mrs Matthews lied. I was armed with the phone call; I held the truth.

"Do you know who phoned you?"

"Cristina something?"

"So, it wasn't a random person it was actually a police officer." I huffed; she was very inconsistent with her evidence. Cristina would have known about the fire and so that wasn't suspicious, so I was back at square one in figuring out what had happened. "I'll ask one final time…" I was getting impatient with her dodging the question. "How did you react."

"The same as anyone would finding out the love of their life had been murdered."

"Which is?"

"I cried, I screamed his name. I felt the world come crashing down on top of me, I wanted it all to have been a dream. I was hoping it was some sick lie someone had planned, that he wasn't dead at all, that he was waiting for me at home. He was waiting for me to walk through the door, for the relief to overtake me, for me to learn that he was better than ok. He was waiting for me to tell him how much I loved him. He was waiting. But he wasn't. I got home and there was no home, nothing but ash. My house was being searched; blue flashing lights lit up the whole street. He was really gone." Her eyes began to flood, I wasn't falling for her trickery. I know a good actor when I see one.

"Can you name the people on this trip in case they need to be questioned?"

"My client doesn't need to do that." That was the most I ever heard him speak. For a lawyer he wasn't doing a good job at defending the suspect.

"If she doesn't it will harm her defence."

"No comment." She decided to take the easy way out, she hadn't run it past the people before dragging them into her mess. By naming them it would link their name to the case and had they not been groomed to tell the correct story there was the chance they could slip up and expose her, something she couldn't afford to do. Juno seemed to be acting a lot more suspicious than Hayley in this moment which led me to believe there was something Juno was hiding. Something wasn't adding up.

"What do you do for a living?"

"I'm a barista."

"Would you say you spend a lot of time at work? I ask because Mr. Matthews seemed to be unemployed for a while, one of you must have been earning money to pay for your flat right?"

"I'm there every day from seven in the morning to half five in the evening. We can afford the flat because we have money from his parents, my wages go on food, clothes and things."

"So, you don't pay rent... it seems perfect. Had you had any arguments recently?" I wondered if she had caught onto where these questions were heading, if she hadn't, I thought for sure her lawyer had.

"Not that I can remember, nothing worth anything."

"So, what else could have inspired you to commit such a horrendous crime?" I knew asking up front wasn't really the best way to go but I couldn't sit and listen to her fabricated truth any longer.

"I didn't do anything... I wasn't even there." For the first time in the whole interview, I believed her, not completely but there was a fragment of trust beginning to emerge.

"Thank you for coming, I may need to talk to you again in a few days, because of the nature of this case we thought it best to keep the suspects here until proven innocent."

The guard escorted Juno out as he had done with Hayley.

Had I just caught the murderer of my final case?

Probably not.

I looked around the empty room wondering what happened on that phone call. What was said that wasn't caught on the train's cameras? It didn't take long before I gave into temptation, I pressed play on the voice recorder, the call began.

Juno: Hey, what is it?

Voice: Goodbye

Juno: Ben?

Ben: I'm sorry.

Juno: What is it?

The recording stopped. I sat in shock for a few minutes, this was nowhere near what I was expecting.

Suicide?

No.

There is no way. He had too much good going on for him to do something like that.

Something still wasn't adding up for me. I shuddered as I stopped the recording for the night and closed my file. Interrogation was over but the case was far from solved.

Before going home that night I stopped by the main office to review any new evidence, a small pile of papers sat in the corner awaiting me I picked them up carefully and slid them into my bag.

Chapter 5

I didn't sleep that night; I went through each piece of evidence. I spent hours drawing up different scenarios none of which led me to the conclusion of suicide. He was just about to start his new job in town, he didn't display any changes in mood, no indications of anything like this... nothing. It really was making less and less sense as time went on. I needed to know more about how Ben was acting before the fire, maybe he was displaying signs, and no one noticed. Perhaps it was a suicide after all.

I thought back to the interrogations, none of the suspects seemed one hundred percent innocent. They

SPARKS OF BETRAYAL

were both somewhat suspicious. Had they worked together? But that still doesn't answer the question of how and why they would set the house alight. At the end of the day, it was Juno's house too, had she started the fire herself she would have had nowhere to stay. Hayley lived with a group of artists in a tiny house with a miniature garage there was no way there was enough space for another one.

I opened my bedside drawer and picked out my black folder, inside was my notebook. I wrote up a list of questions to ask Juno, I needed to know if anything different had happened recently, or maybe if she had finally had enough and snapped. She wasn't going to admit to the murder though, even if she did have something to do with it. How could I work around this strategically? Everything about confronting her seemed wrong... I had to find a different approach. My usual nasty demeanour had to be taken away, I had to learn to judge less but sometimes when you're face to face with a possible murderer you can't help but get frustrated, especially if they refuse to communicate. I knew my job meant that I had to review the situation before judging the person but after almost thirty years I decided for my final case these people are guilty until proven innocent and at the moment none of them were helping themselves.

JUPITER

I went back through the interrogations hoping to spot something that gave the murderer away, it proved to be much more difficult than this, it was exactly how I remembered, nothing new stood out this time. I rummaged through again hoping for something more. Nothing... there just simply wasn't enough yet.

I left the folder on my bed and began piecing together an approach that would lead me to the truth of Juno and Ben's relationship... I started by writing the main questions. I closed my notebook and sighed. The sunrise caught my eye, I stared out of the window as the sky lit up in pink and the dark night faded away. I slipped the folder and my notebook into my bag and headed back to the station.

"Good morning, to you too." I replied. "Is the room free for six?"

"It is." he smiled, "you got another suspect for the Ben Matthews case?"

I turned to the guard, "Could you get suspect B ready for 6am please." he nodded.

"Not exactly." I walked through into the break room, the officer followed. "I've got more to ask Juno." I started the coffee machine and picked my cup out of the tray, placing it in the machine.

SPARKS OF BETRAYAL

"The wife?" he seemed surprised. "Well... actually now you mention it they did seem quite weird the other day."

"Weird in what way?" I asked, if he had any information I needed to know and I needed to know now.

"Well, you know... just weird." He shrugged his shoulders, "I can't really explain it."

"What's your name... In case I have to write it in for evidence."

"Why would you –" he stopped himself. "Dylan."

"Dylan?"

"Officer Jones" he corrected.

"Thank you." I looked at the clock, twenty minutes until I would be face to face with Juno again. I picked up my coffee and made my way to the table. I sat closest to the wall so I could lean my head on it. I opened my notebook to the page full of questions. Dylan didn't move. I flipped to a new page and added the title 'Officer Dylan Jones'. "Do you have anything more than 'acting weird'?" I asked ready to write everything he said. For extra evidence, I started recording from my phone which I placed face down on the table.

"Well, there had been complaints about the noise some said it was music others claimed it was arguing so I don't

JUPITER

know if they were trying to block out the noise of arguments with loud music." he said.

"And you kept this vital information from me because?" I caught sight of the guard through the window, I gave him a nod to tell him to get Juno ready.

"Because I could lose my position."

"Really?" I laughed. "you kept this a secret because your scared of losing your job..."

"It's more than that."

"How do you mean?" I questioned. I put the pen down thinking he'd be more open with me knowing I wasn't keeping a note of his words.

He came closer, "I went over a few times but every time there was no noise so I –"

"So, you what!?" I was becoming increasingly impatient with every word he said, there were five minutes until I had to be with Juno and this information was absolutely crucial in solving the case.

"So, I left" he said quietly as he looked at the floor.

"YOU LEFT?" I screamed.

"Shhh, look... I'm not proud of what I've done. If I could go back and fix it, I would but I can't, and this job is the only good thing for me right now."

SPARKS OF BETRAYAL

"You're expecting sympathy?" I scoffed. "A man is dead... a death that may have been prevented had you just knocked on the door. Do you understand how serious this is?"

"Of course, I do, how could you even suggest that I don't..."

"I should report this..." I panicked.

"No." he pleaded. "Please Meryl this is the only thing I've got."

I sat for a moment staring at this pathetic man. There was not an ounce of regret in his face. If I had to guess I would say there was no remorse in his heart either, as long as he keeps his job, as long as he doesn't get found out. His eyes filled with tears as he tried to make me sympathize. I wasn't going to be tricked... I knew better than that.

His eyes wandered down to my phone, and I followed them with mine his pleading turned to anger as I snatched the phone off the table. I could see a storm building behind his eyes, and a slight panic set in. There was no way I could have known what he was going to do, I could have guessed but what's the use in that? I didn't know what he was capable of. With him being an officer, I figured he'd be strong, I couldn't take my eyes off him... He didn't expect me not to record what he was saying, did he? I mean seriously? I didn't stop the recording, instead, I shoved the phone into my pocket. He grabbed my hair and pulled me down off the chair. His desperation was clear, he was going to do anything and everything to get this recording deleted.

"What the fuck is happening!" Cristina stormed through the door.

I sighed with relief, not because I wasn't strong enough to fight him on my own but because I needed someone else to witness what he was doing. I don't think Dylan heard her through his anger, either that or he enjoyed the audience. He didn't seem so fragile over his job anymore as he threw some punches towards my face, it would have been easier for him to have left the recording. That way he could have avoided an assault charge, now there's no doubt he'll lose his job. He held on, grabbing towards my pocket. I zipped the pocket shut and held it tightly. He breathed heavily. I kicked him off me, he forced his way back. He tried to punch again but I moved, this seemed to anger him even more. He held me down. He clenched his fist to try punching me one more time. I closed my eyes preparing for the impact. Nothing. Instead, the weight holding my legs to the floor was lifted as Cristina dragged him off me. I sat in awe. I stared at her as she dragged him out. The man tried to run but she held on, she struggled to get him out of the door. They both exited the room as I sat in shock for a few seconds.

SPARKS OF BETRAYAL

I looked up at the clock. 6:10am. I was supposed to be in that interrogation room ten minutes ago... I brushed myself down and ran my fingers through my hair to get the tangles out. I picked up my notebook and my bag and made my way out the door. I took my phone out of my pocket and stopped the recording.

"Sorry Meryl," the guard said. "The room is occupied."

I released a sigh of relief. I don't think I could have handled the interrogation after that. "Thank you," I said. I turned to walk away. "Hey, do you know anything about that officer?"

"He wriggled his way free of Cristina's arms, we tried to catch him, but he was too fast."

"Had you ever seen him before?"

"Oh, yeah he comes in sometimes to give me files to pass onto you, just broke up with his wife. It's a shame really, they were a cute couple."

"Ah, okay... how come I've never seen him before?"

"I have no idea," he replied. "Maybe because he gives me all the cases for you, there's no need for him to see you really."

Chapter 6

Steph knocked on the door, returning with my food. If I'm completely honest reading all about that case again made me lose my appetite but I didn't want to hurt Steph's feelings after she'd gone to all that trouble getting it for me.

In her hands was a tray of hospital made cottage pie. I couldn't really complain as cottage pie sat second on my list of favourite meals, just below lasagne but just above macaroni and cheese but I'd never tried it from a hospital canteen. Just the smell was more than enough to put me off food for life.

SPARKS OF BETRAYAL

She placed it on a table above my lap and stepped away.

"I wasn't sure if you wanted gravy, so I brought some up in a small pot." Steph said, holding up a small pot of what looked like dirty water.

"No thank you." Usually, I would never turn down gravy, especially with mashed potato but what Steph was holding was practically water. I took a couple of mouthfuls, it was vile. No one could tell me that people sit and enjoy this kind of food, but I suppose I was going to have to get used to it at some point. I took bigger mouthfuls to try and get rid of it as fast as I could, it was practically tasteless, and the textures were clashing painfully.

"So... was the case interesting?" Steph asked, breaking the silence.

"I need to reopen it I think,"

"Reopen the case?" She sounded shocked.

"Yes" I said.

"What on Earth would make you do that?"

"I'm a fifty-five-year-old woman stuck in a hospital bed... I was given this case twenty years ago and it's still unsolved." I smiled.

"Not all cases get solved."

JUPITER

"Steph... I spent thirty years in the police force, 27 of those as a detective. I've had over a hundred cases handed to me... I've solved every single one, except Ben Matthews. I need this case to be solved because what else do I have?"

"I just don't know if reopening this case is a good idea." Steph sighed. "There's no new evidence, you'll be stuck in the exact same place as you were." I stared at my folder as she spoke, I understood what she was saying but I couldn't understand why finding the truth was such a bad idea.

"You really want to drag all that back up, with Hayley and Juno. What if they don't want it solved anymore, maybe they've finally come to terms with not knowing."

I thought for a second about what she said. She was right... I didn't want to be the one to drag everything up but at the same time it's my job. It's my job to learn the truth, to give people closure, I had done it for every other family, why couldn't I do it for Juno?

"I'll ask Cristina what she thinks."

"Good idea." Steph took my hand and began unravelling the bandages. I looked away. I thought of Cristina, if I could get her to reopen the case with me, she could help me... she'd be here every day. I could see her every day. I smiled. I didn't even care that Cristina's company may be a distraction, all I could think bout was her sitting in the chair next to me.

"I've got to sit you up to redress your back, okay?"

I nodded. This was the worst part of every day. I pushed my legs into the mattress. I closed my eyes tightly. I refused to show my vulnerability even now, I'm a detective I can't afford to be vulnerable. Criminals thrive on vulnerability, you let your guard down even for a second and they fool you. I'm not saying Steph is a criminal, but you never really know what someone has done or is planning to do.

"You can lay back down again." She said, moving down towards my legs. I held my breath; this was the most effective pain relief method so far... She began unbandaging my legs, I couldn't think of anything other than the feeling of every fibre touching my legs, the rest of my body had stopped hurting as much, and the bandages were to minimize the risk of infection; something I desperately needed to do if I was to get out on time. I had been in the hospital less than a week and I already felt the need to leave; I was a busy woman I needed to carry on. I may have retired, but that never stopped people from coming to me for help with all sorts of different cases. As Steph put the new bandages on the pain was inescapable, the more I moved and resisted the worse it was. Holding my breath wasn't doing anything anymore as it got worse and worse the longer it went on. It felt like she was stabbing me with flaming knives. I had experienced excruciating pain in the past but never like this. She finally finished, there were tears in my eyes, but I refused to let them out.

What would Steph think?

I stared at the ceiling thinking of the evidence I had just revised. Finally, something stood out... Dylan. Dylan was an officer; he had the uniform. If it's the same Dylan who dragged me from the fire, there's a lie coming from him somewhere. Was he a fireman or an officer? I needed to find out.

Steph washed her hands in the corner sink and walked towards the door.

"Steph."

"Yes flower." She turned back towards me, "what can I do for you?"

"Do you know where Dylan is?"

"I do." She smiled.

"Could you ask him to come and see me, don't tell him why and maybe bring Cristina too if you can."

"Not a problem." She left the room.

As I waited, I ran through possible questions in my head.

What do you do for a living?

SPARKS OF BETRAYAL

Do you remember what you did to me?

I stopped. As an officer, he said his surname was Jones, but he never told me that… that's where we start. Deciding whether he is the same, Dylan. If he was, we needed to get to the bottom of why he lied about being a fireman. If not, we leave him alone and apologize for wasting his time, but I wasn't letting him go until I investigated every possibility, for all I know he could have killed Ben.

They stepped into the room and closed the door, Dylan sat closer to me which annoyed me slightly.

"I have a question for you." I said.

"Yes?" He said sliding uneasily deeper into the chair, he was making himself look so suspicious and I wasn't sure if he could tell.

"What's your surname?"

"Jones." He replied confidently, I'll be honest it wasn't a hard question. By his reaction, I think he was expecting something harder to answer than that. I wonder what he did to make him so nervous. "Why? Are you considering proposing? You're just checking you like my name for when you take it?" *I despise men.* I sighed. *How embarrassing.*

What would have ever given him that impression?

JUPITER

Cristina laughed, Dylan didn't know why, and we decided not to tell him.

"What? I saved you, isn't that my reward?"

"Get your head out of storybooks, you sound pathetic." Cristina shut him down.

"Moving on," I sighed. "And what was it you said you did for a living?" I asked.

"Fireman," again he answered with such confidence as if he was expecting a reward for knowing the answer.

"Were you ever part of the police force... an officer perhaps?"

His expression shifted. "Who have you been talking to?"

"So that would be a yes..."

He looked as though I had said something he wasn't prepared for and that meant we may finally be getting somewhere.

"So," I said, ready for the real fun to begin. "I'm not going to record you this time, I have nothing." I held my bandaged hands up. "Feel free to search the room, there is nothing recording you." I kept going hoping Cristina would get the hint to start recording. Dylan stood, he looked under the bed and in the drawers. I looked at Cristina, she looked at me. I stopped. Her piercing blue eyes caught me again. She looked down at her phone and began the voice recorder. She placed the phone in the pocket of her blazer. I smiled.

"Are you satisfied?"

He nodded.

"Good," I said. "Are you ready to begin?" I wasn't really giving him a choice; he was doing this whether he liked it or not.

Chapter 7

My eyes locked with his for a moment, unsure where to start.

"Do you remember who I am, do you remember what happened the last time we met?"

He nodded.

"Yes?"

"Yes." He answered quietly. Cristina nodded at me to signal that it was loud enough for the recording.

"Last time I spoke to you... you confessed something, right?"

SPARKS OF BETRAYAL

"I did." He sat, ashamed. I bet he thought I'd forgotten about it all.

"What was it?" I narrowed my eyes. I knew what it was of course I did but I needed to hear him say it again.

"I was given something to investigate and –"

"And what?" Cristina questioned.

"I didn't, I left the house without investigating it." He couldn't look at me.

"You left! You just left?" Cristina exclaimed, "you're only job was to investigate, that's what you were paid to do."

"So, why didn't you investigate the scene?" I asked to calm the situation. I hadn't told Cristina any of this, so she was very much in the dark.

"There were noise complaints, I got there... there was no noise, so I figured it was all okay." He said, "and I get that it was wrong, and I should have knocked anyway... I should have checked, and I know that."

"Well, since you confessed all those years ago, I went through all your records, every report you've ever written. It wasn't just that one time you abandoned the scene, was it?"

"No." He looked down at the ground. I honestly couldn't believe how much he was telling us, maybe because he trusted me not to be able to record. But I was... I was recording it all. I looked over at Cristina who was hearing this for the first time, her eyes were wide with disbelief at what Dylan was saying. I could tell she wanted to scream at us both, him for what he did and me for keeping it from her.

"What did you think as you drove away? Surely, you knew it was wrong before you even left the scene?" I found myself becoming more invested in the story as the questions went on.

"I knew it was wrong of course I did. I don't know why but I just couldn't get myself to turn around."

I changed the subject slightly, "Why did you attack me?" Cristina looked over at me, that was the first thing that sounded at all familiar to her. I never told her the reason just as I didn't tell her about what Dylan had done. She asked and asked but I never snapped.

"You were recording, I knew you were. You could have reported me, what you had was clear evidence that would have gotten me fired as soon as anyone heard what had happened. I had to get it off you, I know I went about it in the worst possible way but once I felt Cristina pull me off you, I panicked. I wasn't about to get an assault charge... just another reason for them to fire me, I couldn't do it. I handed in my notice that evening."

"Your notice?" I was shocked, "but you said you needed that job, why did you throw it away?"

SPARKS OF BETRAYAL

He stared at me for a few seconds, "you had evidence to destroy me. Imagine being fired by the police force I'd never be hired anywhere again, and after hurting you I could have even been facing a criminal record, I wasn't going to risk it." He took the easy way out; I could have still reported him I chose not to. I thought he really needed the job I was willing give him a pass this once, I was late and preoccupied by the ongoing case, I hadn't slept so I just let it go.

"They didn't accept my notice, I never left, they needed me."

"They don't get a choice on accepting a notice or not, only you can withdraw it. So, you must have, it doesn't matter now there's no point getting caught up in that." I looked down at the file, "when I came here... you said you were a fireman." I remembered, "are you?"

"No, I was hoping you didn't remember me." I couldn't believe it; he was appearing more and more suspicious as the questions went on... Why was he doing this to himself? There was no way I wasn't reopening the case with this new information... he doesn't know why he left the house unchecked? He had something to do with it all I know it... Yet again, nothing was making sense there were just too many missing pieces. "Please don't report me now, surely it's been too long, please I'm happy now."

JUPITER

He's happy now?

That's what he cares about...

That he's happy.

"Can I ask something..." Cristina interjected. I nodded. "I get that the house and the whole leaving the scene situation is significant for Dylan but is there any reason you're bringing it up now?"

"It was Ben Matthew's house."

Her expression flipped; her confusion faded to shock. Everything finally slotted into place for her. "Wait... you're not reopening the case, are you?"

"We could... I mean, I wanted to." I stared at the ceiling to avoid making any eye contact. I didn't think any of them would approve. Dylan wouldn't if he was at all guilty, and by what I have now I may just be able to prove it. Cristina was staring at me I could feel it, but was she angry or prepared? I couldn't keep from looking at her. She's so beautiful even when she's angry.

"Meryl it's been years... you want to drag it all back up?"

"I want to find the truth." I said defensively as she was the second to suggest I was doing it with bad intentions. Quite frankly I was offended that they saw me that way.

A knock on the door interrupted the disagreement. Steph walked in.

SPARKS OF BETRAYAL

"I think it's best Meryl gets some rest." She looked at Dylan and Cristina. They stood and made their way to the door.

"Cristina?" I called, "can you come back tomorrow?"

"Of course, I can," she smiled. I caught one final glimpse of her eyes before she left me for the night.

"Do you need anything before I go home?" Steph asked, "I'll be back in the morning."

"No, thank you Steph." I smiled. She nodded before turning to the door.

I was back to being alone. I pushed myself down back to lying flat, no one was there so I finally allowed myself to react to the pain. I breathed heavily and close my eyes tightly, there was nothing I could do about it I just needed to wait it out. I fidgeted for a while unable to find a comfortable position, only making it worse. I finally got comfortable, laying on my back exactly as I was before.

I stared up at that same spot on the ceiling, my mind flooded with thoughts of Cristina.

JUPITER

Chapter 8

Cristina, Cristina, Cristina, Cristina, Cristina,

Cristina, Cristina, Cristina, Cristina, Cristina,

Cristina, Cristina, Cristina, Cristina, Cristina,

Cristina, Cristina, Cristina, Cristina, Cristina,

Cristina, Cristina, Cristina, Cristina, Cristina,

Cristina, Cristina, Cristina, Cristina, Cristina,

Chapter 9

I couldn't stop thinking about her. Her eyes... Her ice blue eyes. Her hair was short and dark, the brown colour of wood when the autumn rain falls. Her skin was fair and perfect, she was fifty-six, but you'd never guess by her face.

How dare she be so perfect.

She was the one I fantasized about making memories with. The one I'd fill scrapbooks with, we'd have hundreds of polaroid pictures of all our adventures tied into a perfectly decorated book with titles and notes in Cristina's perfect handwriting. She was the one I wanted to help me decorate the Christmas tree, her creativity was far better than mine and her decorations always shone brighter. everything was also placed meticulously with every colour complimenting the others. I never will understand how her brain works but I'd give anything to be let into even just a tiny bit of her amazing mind. I ~~wanted~~ want to be with her until the end. Maybe I wasted my chance... Maybe I was too focused on work, I was too focused on not letting a relationship get in the way of my success. I've known forever — that she was the one, but I was just so focused on my career I pushed it all away... I pushed her away.

Now, I lay, with my whole life behind me still chasing that same girl. I trust her with my life, I would give my life for her. I've never trusted anyone before, not like this. I was closed off to all that bullshit I didn't need anyone, I'd seen too much betrayal when it came to trusting people I made a promise to myself that I would never let myself trust another human being. It was simply too risky, but here she is. It seems she has the key to my lock, she is the one.

My lip quivered; my eyes flooded with tears knowing I was never going to have her.

We would never have our own home. Somewhere where we could make autumn cookies, somewhere out of town, somewhere quiet. Somewhere we could grow old. She would never want something like that with

SPARKS OF BETRAYAL

someone like me. I let the tears fall off my face onto the pillow beneath me.

Why didn't she want me?

I sighed, I had no choice, I couldn't ask her now she had settled. She has a home...she makes autumn cookies... she decorates her tree... it's just not with me.

I could imagine as much as I wanted but the reality will always be that I was never good enough for her. She deserved someone beautiful, someone kind and open, not someone covered in scars and deeply mistrusting, she deserved a hundred times better than me. She deserves the world and that seems to be something I just can't give.

I was only ever brave enough to ask her out once. I invited her into my mind and once I was rejected I never opened it up for anyone else.

***

Graduation came and I just had to ask, what if I never saw her again? This was one of my biggest regrets because not only did she reject me she ended up working with me, we were platonically inseparable. Don't get me wrong it was amazing getting to spend that much time with someone you cared about but at the same time listening to her gush lovingly about her girlfriend got rather frustrating. I couldn't lose her as a friend we had been together too long for me to throw that away. I dated a couple of girls from town but something was missing... Her. None of them came close to her, my love was reserved for her. I should have been more careful, falling for my best friend, what was I thinking?

It's one of the easiest things to do but it's dangerous. You don't know when but before long that's it, you're trapped. Your mind floods with things they've said, things they've done and there's no escaping it. Fighting the feelings will only take you so far. You have no control over it. Every time you see them, your mind is screaming, you want them to know but you just can't bring yourself to say anything.

There's no easy way out of falling for your best friend, it either ends in a relationship you're too afraid to ruin because of all the expectations you build over the years of friendship or you are left to suffer the gut wrenching pain of watching them move on with someone else knowing that it could have been you.

The risk with Cristina was far too great for me to take, had anything happened I couldn't face the loss. I refused to lose her.

Years go by, you see them every day and, nothing changes. You say nothing, your mind is still screaming for their attention every second that they're with you.

SPARKS OF BETRAYAL

You stay and wonder whether they will ask you first, but those words never come from them. The never say it, and so you don't either.

Falling for your best friend... It'll only break your heart.

Cristina was the luckiest of us two, she ended up with a girl perfect for her, she was nothing like me.

She settled quickly after graduating, they've been together now 33 years, they got married but it was nothing special. Just everyday clothes in a small hotel, I never quite understood why. She said it was to save money to travel but they hadn't really been anywhere. They're inseparable even now. I'm nothing compared to her and I wouldn't dream of coming between them. I'm forced to watch from the side lines. Although it's not my perfect situation I get to see her smile.

***

By now there was a small puddle of tears accumulated on my pillow, a reminder that I'm alone and the love of my life is at home with hers. I decided to try getting some sleep before I sent myself into an endless pit of yearning.

Chapter 10

The morning approached a lot faster than I thought it would. I had barely closed my eyes for a second before Steph was bringing me breakfast.

"Morning," the tray supported a buttered croissant, a banana and some orange juice. "I got your breakfast."

"I'm starting to think you can read my mind," I laughed. "Usually no one can pick out foods I like even if I tell them."

She smiled as she put the tray on the table above my lap. "Lucky guesses." She stepped away and opened the

SPARKS OF BETRAYAL

blinds, the bright sun shone through the window. I'd do anything to be out there right now.

"Is Cristina coming today?"

"She is, she told me to tell you she'll be late she had to take Yvette to work."

Yvette could drive, there were buses I couldn't understand why Cristina had started taking her?

I stopped myself... what right did I have questioning their relationship?

I smiled, hiding what I was really feeling, Steph would be disappointed with me if she knew. They'd all know how jealous I am of her happy ever after.

"Someone else is here to see you though and after yesterday you absolutely have the right to turn him away." She said, pointing at Dylan who had the audacity to walk back through those doors.

"What are you doing?" I laughed, hoping what I was seeing was a lie.

"I wanted to apolo—"

"Apologize?" I scoffed, there's no way I heard that correctly.

He nodded sheepishly. "I—" he stopped to choose his words, that was never a good sign when dealing with a

JUPITER

possible murderer. It could mean a multitude of things, he was remembering his premade script, thinking back to what will get him out of trouble. He could have been telling the truth, it could have been that he just wanted to get the wording right. The most realistic explanation in my mind was that he was lying, especially considering everything I've learnt in the past. I shuddered awaiting his response.

"I want you to know, I had nothing to do with either fire."

I looked at Steph, she shrugged.

"Could you tell him to leave please." I said, "You're lucky I haven't been able to reopen the case yet."

Steph escorted him out closing the door behind him. She looked over at me, I wasn't sure how much of the story she knew by now as I can't remember whether she was in the room... I don't think she was, but why would Steph say *after yesterday*? Could she hear us?

"Steph?" I squinted slightly to see her face, "how much do you know from yesterday?"

"Nothing really, but Dylan left the room with anger in his eyes, saying he had been exposed or something? Told me to tell the police you were lying if you decided to talk to them about him."

That seemed suspicious even for Dylan, he had nothing to lose anymore. If all he was worried about was his job

SPARKS OF BETRAYAL

and reputation he was in the clear. He's practically retired and if it's the assault charge he's worried about then he's being ridiculous. He and I both know there's no point dragging up a case from over two decades ago, this is true for all except the Ben Matthews case, I simply couldn't let that one go. If I'm being completely honest I believe he's hiding much more. He has something to do with the murder of Ben Matthews, I know it. Until now I hadn't joined the dots between Ben's fire and my own. That would mean whoever tried to kill Ben tried to get rid of me too, that's why they locked the door. Maybe it was one of the original suspects, they wanted to get rid of me before I figured them out? I just sat for a few seconds and let the thoughts calm down.

"Is everything alright, Meryl?"

"Yeah, sorry I was just thinking." I smiled. "You look immaculate in this sunlight."

"Thank you, Meryl." She seemed genuinely surprised, she blushed. It was true, her dark skin shone beautifully, her golden eyeliner matched the autumn season and her Red lipstick tied it all together, she was beautiful. "If you can excuse the scrubs" she laughed.

"I like your scrubs." I said.

She smiled, she sat beside me resting her arm on the bed.

JUPITER

"Are you okay?" she asked, her expression was completely serious.

"Yeah," I said. I tried to piece together what could have caused this sudden worry, had I let my guard down? Had I been vulnerable? I couldn't afford to be, not now I was so close to being able to reopen the case.

"Meryl, this isn't something small you know... you almost died, it's my duty to make sure you're coping... I know I wouldn't be if it had been me."

I wanted to scream, tell her everything. I wanted my house back; I wanted my life back. I knew if I said anything they'd never let me reopen the case, they'd send me to therapy... I'd avoided it for fifty five years I wasn't going to let this be the thing to send me there. I shuffled around trying to find comfort, I was met still with sharp pain all over.

"I'm fine," I smiled. "I've seen worse, you know being a detective and all."

She nodded, "okay but please talk to me if there is anything."

The door swung open, startling us both. Cristina stood holding her laptop in her arms. "Are we doing this or what?" She smiled.

"I'll leave you two to it shall I?" Steph said.

SPARKS OF BETRAYAL

"You can stay if you want," I said.

"I've got a lot to do and I'm sure you don't need me, Murder isn't my specialty I prefer saving the lives." She giggled as she closed the door.

She was here again, finally sat right next to me, I could have reached out and taken her hand. She opened her laptop to a document she had saved, "This might be of interest to you." She said, turning the laptop around.

A CCTV style video played, it was of Ben. He stood outside his house, talking to another man. They exchanged a cake box, the man then turned to his car and took out some balloons. I couldn't quite make out who it was. The video froze, Cristina turned the laptop back to herself and looked at me.

"I don't understand." I said.

"This was Ben on the day of the fire." She said, "It looks like he was planning a party. You wouldn't set fire to your house if you were planning a party would you?"

"No! No you wouldn't, are you finally suggesting that he didn't do it to himself?" I was relieved that she had finally began seeing the case as I had all those years ago, she was finally on my side.

"Precisely, there's no way."

"But how come the police never saw this footage before?" It seemed quite strange that the police asked for every CCTV footage within a three mile radius and missed one so close.

"I have no idea... I guess they just missed it." She stared at me, "there was no one else around after this, nothing to suggest who it could have been."

"Well we know it wasn't suicide," I knew this all along, I was just waiting for someone to believe me. "We're dealing with murder by arson." As I heard myself say it out loud I wondered whether I had taken on more than I can actual handle.

"We are." She looked down at what very little evidence we had gathered. "Have we taken on too much? Do we maybe need to ask for some help?"

"Help from who?" I exclaimed, "We shouldn't even be doing this I don't think anyone's going to help us, even with this new evidence."

She sat pondering our options, not that there really were any.

"Let's just do as much as we can, if nothing comes up maybe we leave it, maybe it's a case not meant to solved."

"Only if we don't find anything, we need to do something about Dylan though." I said.

SPARKS OF BETRAYAL

"Definitely, he's just too suspicious to let it go. That's where we begin."

I nodded, I couldn't believe she had finally decided to help me. Now that she and I were working on this together I'd see her almost every day. I'd see her almost every day, I said it over and over in my head. A smile spread across my face.

"What?" She laughed.

"Nothing." I lied. My eyes wandered around the room trying to avoid eye contact. I couldn't have her finding me out before we even start.

"No, what is it?"

I froze. I couldn't tell her that I was imagining us both driving around the world trying new foods from every country or that every time I saw her my heart skipped a beat. I couldn't tell her any of that. "I'm just glad you decided to help me."

"Of course, I'm going to help you."

"You didn't seem too keen in the beginning." I reminded her, she's acting like it was her plan all along but it wasn't she looked at me like I was stupid when I suggested it the first time.

"That's only because well, let's be honest it sounded stupid to begin with." At least she was being honest I suppose. "Sorry I reacted like that, I'm ready now."

I felt bad for making her apologize but the way her words made sentences made the butterflies in my stomach go insane. I had to stop thinking about her like this... it's so unprofessional. How are we ever going to get anything done?

"Have you got anything else?" I asked, looking down at the folder. "I had just gone through the first interrogations, I still need to read Juno's second one."

"Well then let's start there." She shuffled closer so she could see the papers. I felt her warm breath on my wrists. Her rose perfume scent returned.

Chapter 11

When I finally got to the interview room it had gone dark outside, the whole day was wasted, there was no more evidence, we were nowhere nearer to the answer and there was only time for a twenty minute interrogation. I brushed my blazer down and corrected the collar on my shirt before stepping into the room.

JUPITER

Juno – 21:40 – Friday 10th November 2000.

"Hello Juno." I was still trying to find a way to approach the situation. I sat opposite the suspect. "I just have a couple more questions for you."

She looked up, she said nothing.

"Seeming as there was no cause found, can you think of anything that could have sparked the blaze?"

"Nothing, he wasn't one for candles. They made him uncomfortable. He wouldn't have left anything over a heater, he wouldn't have done it."

"Were not saying he did it we're just wondering if there's a plausible explanation before we start rummaging for a murder suspect." I realised there may have been an accidental reason for the fire, I should have asked this before jumping to conclusions. I had never done that before... I was always thorough before throwing accusations around. Why was it different this time?

I couldn't have my career end on an accident, and I knew that was a horrid thing to think but what am I supposed to do. I've been given the most dramatic, exciting and disturbing cases in the country and this is what I end on... an accident? Someone reading in a candle lit room and knocking over the candle, burning the pile of books?

SPARKS OF BETRAYAL

My thoughts ran away from the interrogation, I didn't know what to ask anymore I was completely lost for words. What kind of monster was I turning into?

"Why did it take so long for someone to phone the fire brigade?" She switched the questioning towards me, I was completely unprepared. I couldn't answer her, I wasn't there how was I supposed to know?

"I I don't know" I stuttered, how else do I respond?

"What do you mean you don't know?" I understood she wanted answers but surprisingly I really wasn't the person to ask. "The house was engulphed in bright orange flames and you mean to tell me no one noticed, it's a house in the middle of town for goodness sake!"

I didn't know what to say. It did seem strange that there were that many people in the town and not one of them thought to phone for help? Unless they did and there was a delay? This is what was going to lead me to the next piece of evidence, I needed to find out when they were notified, when they arrived, who notified them? This was all crucial information, why hadn't the police gone through it all yet? I needed to find the main officer on the case.

Wasting this interrogation time was out of the question so I continued asking about the relationship between herself and Ben Matthews.

"Was anything different, in terms of yours and Mr Matthew's relationship?"

"No," she said defensively. "Everything was as it should be."

"Okay, we're just trying to figure out what happened." I calmed my voice, "we had some noise complaints a few days prior to the fire is all."

"Did you?"

"You didn't know?"

"No," she looked up, refusing to let the tears exit. "Why didn't anyone tell us, don't the police usually come to investigate?"

"Yes, that's a separate issue right now that officer is being punished." I lied, he'd ran off we didn't know where he was.

"If only you'd have come in." She avoided every opportunity for eye contact, I became slightly suspicious of her refusing to look at me.

"What do you mean by that?"

"If only they'd stepped in... he used to get angry a lot and well that usually turned into hitting me, but he didn't mean it. He never meant to do it he just couldn't control himself sometimes." I'm not sure what I was expecting from this case but it certainly wasn't that. "He'd do it ns of betrayal

SPARKS OF BETRAYAL

nearly every day for an hour or so after coming home from work, and I know how suspicious I'm making myself look believe me I do, a wife abused by her husband leads to murder but please believe me that's not what happened at all."

"Why didn't you tell anyone?"

"They'd have taken him away from me. I told someone once and they promised, and they've never broken a promise before." By now streams of tears were dripping down her face, I reached to my tissues offering them to her. I had no idea any of this was happening and I would see Ben every day at work. He was one of us... he was exposed to so much violence that may have been a factor, he'd come into work deal with so much and well, he had to get that anger out somewhere.

"Was this every day?"

"Near enough," she whispered. "I'd always put it down to him having had a bad day at work, he hated himself afterwards." Perhaps we were dealing with a suicide after all, I mean he didn't mean to hurt her, he couldn't control himself the only way he could see to stop was stopping altogether.

"Thank you Juno, do you have anywhere to stay tonight?"

JUPITER

"One of Hayley's friends are out of town I'm having her room for a while." She explained.

"Let us know if we can do anything else." I smiled. "You're free to go." She left the room, I shuddered.

I sat for a second, could we prove what she was saying was true? Would it have been self defence or was she facing a minimum thirty five year prison sentence?

I stood up, ready to leave for the night, the guard stood outside waiting for me.

"We may be dealing with more than we originally thought." I sighed. I walked into the common room, grabbed my coat and headed home. I didn't quite know how to react... What do you do when someone admits to having been exposed to years of abuse... I thought it best to leave her be for a few days, start searching for evidence elsewhere.

Chapter 12

"I wouldn't ever have thought..." She whispered.

"I did. I did think about that, and I thought about whether Dylan could have caught it earlier. We had failed her, we were called and she didn't even know... because he never checked.

Cristina picked up the paper, scanning the interrogation over and over. "Self-defence?"

I shook my head. "She wasn't in town at the time of the fire so unless she got someone to do it for her she had nothing to do with it."

"I looked over at her laptop." Juno was out of town and he was seen taking heart balloons and cake inside... was he planning something nice for her?

"He might have done something to her before she went out... that would explain the cake, maybe it's an apology."

"If he was doing anything like that to me I'd need more of a cake to make it right." I breathed. "Even if he was trying to make it up to her it wouldn't explain how she set fire to the house from that far away it's just impossible."

"Is it safe to rule her out yet though?" Cristina put the paper back into the folder.

"I don't think so, just because she could have easily gotten someone else to do it for her and that would make her far from innocent."

Cristina nodded. I was beginning to get frustrated, we were still no closer to finding who caused the fire. We were just going in circles with the evidence we already had... we needed something more. Something solid. Forensics had held onto the evidence gathered on the day of the fire, there wasn't much to work with but if we could match anything to anyone it could help.

"Forensics?" Cristina suggested as if she'd read my mind.

SPARKS OF BETRAYAL

"Mhm," I agreed.

"I could go now; I'll bring the file back later this afternoon." I checked the time; it had just passed one o'clock.

"Perfect, I'll go through the rest of this." My head bowed down, so I was looking at the thin file. I had seen the forensic results before, but they wanted them back at the university after the police ruled the case as a suicide.

Cristina stood; I grabbed her hand before she walked away.

"But they don't know we've reopened the case."

"I know what I'm doing." Her voice was reassuring, I trusted her.

She walked away; her hair bounced as she did. I smiled; she was amazing. Even just walking away was beautiful. She turned around sharply; I hid my smile.

"I'll be back soon, okay."

I was becoming fed up with how many times I watched people leave, they never stayed for very long and I was left alone again. I couldn't decide whether it was good to be alone, I'd rather have Cristina stay with me than to have her in for an hour or so at a time. I sighed.

I flicked through the file, there wasn't much more. A few aftermath photos stood out; it was mostly grey ash with

JUPITER

very little colour. There wasn't much left of the house. I've seen how fast a house fire can take over but surely someone should have done something to help before it got that bad. It was a busy town on a Saturday, people must have been home, some may have walked past, maybe some even stopped to see what was happening... but no one called for help before the whole house collapsed in on itself.

Chapter 13

I took out the fire station's report, scanning the order and times in which things happened. The information lay before me as follows:

FIRE UNIT 22 received reports of a house fire at 44 Meadow Lane at 21:35.

FIRE UNIT 13 arrived at 21:38 after dealing with a smaller fire just a few moments away.

FIRE UNIT 22 arrived at 21:44.

FIRE UNIT 7 arrived at 21:45.

The fire was completely out by 22:27.

JUPITER

The search for a cause began.

Ben Matthews was found at 22:42.

FIRE UNIT 7 left the scene at 22:45.

FIRE UNIT 22 left the scene at 22:47.

FIRE UNIT 13 left the scene at 23:00

There were eighty five minutes between when the call was made, and the final fire engine left the scene. There was only three minutes between when the call was made and when they arrived at the scene... there was just no plausible explanation for how the house was so far gone before anything was done. The fire brigade wasn't too far away, should they have noticed the bellowing smoke? Would they have seen it from where they were? I couldn't make sense of any of it. Unless they're backs were all turned to the blaze there was simply no way they wouldn't have noticed.

I considered my options. I had a journal entry from one of the first firefighters on scene, Yvette Roberts, but I also needed some more witnesses. Was it too late to contact the person who called for help? How would I even get hold of them without getting caught? I wouldn't even know how to ask for the archive calls without going through a hierarchy of different officers, none of which can know what I'm doing.

SPARKS OF BETRAYAL

I sighed; I was getting nowhere. The evidence I needed would be hidden away somewhere if only I'd never let them close the case. I stared back up at the ceiling, and my mind stopped. I wanted the case to go away, I needed answers, but the search is infuriating, I can't go anywhere, and I can't do anything, this is the only thing keeping me occupied but I don't want to spend another month searching just to find nothing more than we already have. I knew I was missing some pieces from the case, some were taken and given to the university criminal justice department, and some had been taken back to the station. I had mostly only photocopies in my file simply because it was unsolved. If anything, new was found it would have been added to the station case but nothing new came to light in almost fifteen years.

I looked back down at what I had, there must be something I'm missing.

JUPITER

Chapter 14

We were at the scene mere moments after having the call, even before we were getting ready to go, of course, we could see the smoke it was dark and thick. There was nothing we could do until putting the fire we were dealing with, out first, we thought people would have called for unit 13 which we knew was close by. When we got there it was worse than we imagined, we didn't think it had been burning for nearly as long as it clearly had been, I shuddered as I saw the house collapsing in on itself. There were people screaming for help, people pointing

SPARKS OF BETRAYAL

towards the house in a panic. By the time I removed myself from my seat, every sound had blended into one. The phones mustn't have been working, they wouldn't have just let it burn, I know this town. I watched on as my friends ran in one by one to the fire. I sprayed the house from the road. I only just started working at the fire station, this was the biggest fire I'd ever seen, the biggest fire I think any of us had seen in this small town. The heat from the flames dried my eyes, and as the smoke filled the air, I could hardly see the building. The flames only grew stronger, the firemen that went in had to come out, it was far too dangerous especially since the building was still in the process of falling in on itself. Three women and two men went in and every one of them made it out, I smiled as they ran out into the street. The joy was short lived as more of the house came crumbling, crashing dramatically into the burning soil. There was no flooring left in the house, the wood had turned to ash. Everything had turned to ash, there was nothing left of the house except a couple stubborn pieces of wall that would inevitably fall with the rest. I couldn't believe what I was seeing, had we gotten there earlier most of the house could still be standing.

The water kept beating down on the rising flames, we couldn't seem to calm it down. It was swiftly approaching the neighboring houses. After what felt like a lifetime weakening the flames, they finally calmed.

JUPITER

I sighed, I walked closer to the pile of ash, the last pieces of wall crumbled as the final flame died. I kept dampening the ash for a few seconds to make sure every flame was extinguished. The water turned off and I stood in shock, I had passed the house that morning on the way to work. The police and fire departments began their investigation, my gaze fixed on the floor.

Muffled speaking filled my head, I couldn't piece together what anyone was saying until Cristina said, "Do we know if everyone was out of the house?"

That's when I remembered. I completely froze, my head filled with noise, not speaking, sirens, screaming or roaring flames, it was a kind of static... almost silent but there was so much noise.

Cristina tapped me on the shoulder, I heard her voice softened, "was Ben inside?"

I couldn't speak my throat dried, my breathing became heavy, my gaze still fixed on the pile of ash presented in front of us. She rested her hand on my shoulder, my silence may have given her the answer she needed. She tried pulling me away from the scene, but my legs wouldn't move, it was as if they were glued to the ground. She just stood, staring at the ruins. My vision blurred. My legs finally moved, I stepped forwards toward the building, and my whole body shook. Cristina grabbed my hand.

SPARKS OF BETRAYAL

"Yvette..." She said, "I think it's best you stay over here. Just in case they find something you don't want to see." She led me back towards the pavement where we sat, waiting for anything.

Time went on and on, minutes felt like hours. I sat patiently on the pavement... I felt completely useless, this was my job, and I was just sitting on the side-lines.

I didn't know what we were expecting to find after that but there couldn't have been much to see but ash.

Finally, after what felt like an eternity, the police walked over to us. Cristina stood; the officer's face was still. Cristina turned to me, her face was that of sympathy, I knew exactly what she was saying. She wasn't the first to have looked at me like that. My legs shook as I fixed my gaze on the house one last time, Ben was gone. He must have been on the way to work; he was in his uniform. All that was left of it was his flameproof jacket and even that was slightly burnt. I shuddered, I knew he must have died a while ago, the heat, the smoke, the building collapsing on top of him. I wondered what did it, what was the final thing that took him? I wanted to assume he didn't suffer much, that it was fast but only he would know. I was infuriated by the fact no one thought to call for help, there really was no reason for him to be dead. If only we got there sooner, if only someone had told us earlier...

Chapter 15

 No one called for help?" I whispered.

"What?" Steph said. I closed the file quickly. Her eyes were fixed on the paper on the table.

"How long have you been here?" My hands shook.

"Not long enough..." She turned her back towards me. "Is that Yvette's journal?"

"Yeah " I paused, "How did you know?"

"I-" She stuttered, "I was there too."

SPARKS OF BETRAYAL

"You were where?" I asked, unsure if she meant the fire or at the time Yvette was writing. I picked up my phone that I had hidden in the file and pressed record.

"All of it, she had been arguing with Cristina all day she went to work at around mid-day. She was obviously doing a late shift because Cristina phoned me asking where she was. I was getting worried because my brain seems to do that when people don't answer for a while. I went on my evening walk around all the places she could be, and I noticed some flames. I assumed they were already there considering the size of the blaze."

"How long did it take you to get to the fire from that point?" I asked.

"No more than two minutes." She shuddered, "no one was there, no blue lights, no sirens, no one was there." Her legs shook beneath her, "No one had called for help." She whispered. Her eyes filled with tears. I didn't want to push her for information, but I needed to know who made that phone call.

"Did you see who did phone the fire brigade?"

"Me." I felt her emotion escape within her breath. She turned towards me, her mask covered her face, but her eyes were full of sadness. She shook her head trying to shake the emotions away.

JUPITER

"I saw Yvette…" she said, "She was stuck… Her face is engraved in my mind. She didn't know what to do, well, what do you do in that situation?" She scoffed, questioning it rather than trying to make sense of it all. I envied her for that, the way she could just accept that there are some things she would never know.

The room fell silent, Steph turned back towards the door, "I'm sorry." She whispered before exiting.

She had nothing to apologize for, I shouldn't have asked. My eyes wandered around the room, there was still something missing. Just a few more pieces of evidence could lead me to reopen the case.

"Is Steph alright?" Cristina asked as she walked into the room with a tray and a bag of evidence. "I brought your food up, it's just a sandwich and some snacks," she smiled.

"Thank you."

She approached my table, the bottom of tray scraped against the uneven surface.

"What have you found?" I asked staring at the bag.

"Some clothes, they matched with Juno, but she did live there so it's not as reliable as we would have hoped."

"Anything else?"

SPARKS OF BETRAYAL

"The door key found outside." She placed it on the table. "It matched with a few suspects but again it wasn't particularly reliable because I picked it up without gloves so traces of me were also found."

"Steph was the one who called for help."

"She was there?" Cristina looked down. "I've been thinking actually and, I really don't think any of this is a good idea I mean there really is nothing more."

I looked back at the slim folder, maybe it was the time just to leave it alone. Not all cases are solved, and it was time I accepted that. I sighed, "okay."

"Okay." Cristina smiled.

"If I leave this case alone, can I have some evidence from another case...?"

"That depends..." I could tell she was skeptical; she had a right to be. I was almost certain she wasn't going to let me go anywhere near what I was about to ask...

"The fire... my house."

"Absolutely not. Why would you even consider that?"

"I cannot sit here anymore not knowing what to do with myself." I felt my voice breaking, my vulnerability was showing, and it infuriated me. I swallowed the lump in my throat, now was not the time to break.

"I'm not going to let you go through evidence of a fire that almost killed you... Meryl you're strong but even you have your limits."

"Cristina, I am the top detective in the country, I can handle a fire."

"I'm not saying you can't... I've seen you do it before. But I can't put you through this, not this one."

"Why not?"

"Are you hearing yourself right now?" She was becoming impatient. "It hasn't even been two weeks."

"Why won't you just –"

"Because I care about you. I don't care what you think. I do care, and I have done since cadets. You used to care about me too."

"I do care –"

"No, you don't." She scoffed. "I rejected you and you lost interest. You never looked at me the way you used to, even now you hardly acknowledge me."

"What are you talking about?"

"You and me!" Her eyes filled with tears, "All I've ever done is cared for you, even now who is sat by you?"

"You rejected me and married Yvette..."

SPARKS OF BETRAYAL

She stopped. Her face shifted, she looked perplexed.

"I never married Yvette."

My heart sank. "What do you mean?"

"I never married her, who told you that?"

"Ben" I whispered.

"He wanted Yvette to marry me, he tried his best to make me propose."

I stared in disbelief. How didn't I know about any of this?

"He did a lot to try, not as bad as what he was doing to Juno, I had a way out. He wanted the best for his sister, I was who he chose but I wasn't who Yvette chose. I was never good enough for her."

Not good enough? Cristina, you are more than enough for anyone, you're absolutely perfect, if she couldn't see that then that's her problem.

Why hadn't anyone reported him before? The more I heard the less I felt I knew Ben. I was overcome with sadness the first time I heard of his death but now... I shuddered. Now I'm not sure how to feel. I wasn't aware of anything. I saw him every day, I'm supposed to be a detective how did I miss it? Suddenly his death was my fault, completely my fault. Every time he hurt Juno, Yvette, or anyone else it was completely my fault. I should have seen right through it all, years upon years

JUPITER

of training and experience in these exact situations and I couldn't even see it right I front of my face. Have those who he hurt turned to hurt him? Are those the suspects?

I shook myself out of my thoughts, Cristina had left, I was on my own again. Just me and my thoughts... exactly how I hated it.

Chapter 16

I just sat in silence for the rest of the day. For the first time since arriving here my head was empty. Silent. I hadn't experienced this before. There was absolutely nothing I could think of. I wanted to think of the cases, but my brain stayed blank. I stared towards the window; I couldn't see through it as the rain drops blurred to view. Steph hadn't returned and I didn't know what was happening with Cristina.

Chapter 17

"You're burns don't seem to be healing fast enough." The doctor said, I heard the words but ignored them. I didn't care anymore. It didn't matter how long I was in here for, I had no purpose. Ben Matthews' case was never going to be solved, Juno was never going to have that feeling of closure and neither was I. I was tied to the fact that I didn't allow Juno to learn the truth. I should never have told Cristina I was reopening the case... I never should have touched that case again; Juno didn't deserve that.

I dragged everything back up and that was worse than living without the answers. I shouldn't have even thought about it. I'd spend my whole life apologizing to her if I could. The guilt held me in a chokehold. It was all my fault. My whole life I had dedicated myself to finding the answers... knowing everything. My final case... I failed.

There must have been something I missed but without a way to check how was I to know? I've checked a hundred times over and still I find nothing.

"Meryl?"

"What?" My voice broke. I looked up, swallowing the emotion that had climbed its way up my throat.

"You're burns don't seem to be healing fast enough." He repeated.

"Okay, what do I do about that?" I said.

"You have a few options but ultimately you'll have to stay here a while longer."

"How much longer?" Not that I even cared anymore.

"Two weeks, perhaps a little more."

"Okay." I said.

"Is everything okay?"

"Of course, it is... why?" I tilted my head as if I was genuinely shocked by his concern.

JUPITER

"Last time I checked you couldn't wait to get out, now you don't want to leave."

"Well things change." I smiled, I left out the part where I don't have a house to go back to or anyone to stay with.

"I suppose they do" he replied.

Chapter 18

The boredom finally hit me. I had been laying in the hospital bed for weeks but only now, only without the Ben Matthews case file did I feel the full force of boredom pushing me downwards. There was only so much I could see out the window although I was allowed to move around now. I wanted to go out in the gardens, but I wanted to go with Cristina. I didn't know when she would return or even if she would ever be back. I didn't have the right to be annoyed at her I shouldn't have pushed for the case, but I had the right to be upset. She's my favourite person in the world, I love her with every bone in my body. It was just a shame she didn't love me back.

I was so frustrated with myself after hearing that she and Yvette weren't even together. I watched them every day at work and they both seemed like the most romantic couple I'd ever seen. If only I'd known it was all an act, a lie, a way for Ben to get his own way. I could have had a chance. I would have had a chance.

Steph stormed through the door without knocking, she had never done that before. I sat up suddenly wondering what had happened to make her burst through with obvious urgency.

"I've got something you might like." Her breath was heavy as if she'd ran up a hundred stairs.

"What is it?"

She held up a small bracelet between her fingers, I recognized it at once.

"Where did you find that!" The words escaped a bit faster than I had expected.

"Shh, no one knows I have it."

"What do you me—"

"It's from – the uhm – the" She stuttered, her eyes fixed on the dangling piece of jewellery, "It's from the fire."

SPARKS OF BETRAYAL

"My fire?" I whispered.

She nodded, and bought it closer to me, it is the exact one I thought it was. I had been looking for it for years. She placed it in my hand.

"It couldn't have been there before the fire," I whispered, "I'd have noticed." I didn't put it on in case they took it away again and I lost it forever. I put it in the small bag of things Cristina had brought in for me.

Chapter 19

"What are you trying to say?"

"I- I don't know."

"You do Steph – You do know." She took a step back, shocked I suppose by my sudden certainty. "You know something. Please just tell me people seem to be keeping too many secrets from me at the moment and I can't take it anymore I just – I can't."

"I just –"

SPARKS OF BETRAYAL

"You just what?" I snapped. I shouldn't have. "I'm sorry," I whispered.

"I don't think the fires were accidental." She said.

I sighed. I can't even begin to describe the relief that accompanied those seven words. I didn't expect anyone to believe me, let alone both Cristina and Steph. I thought I was being stupid, like I was inventing some sort of alternative reality because I couldn't accept that Ben would do anything close to suicide.

"Everyone did." She said, her voice shook. "They thought you were going to go on some revenge mission once you found the first suspect."

"Really?" I scoffed; I knew they thought I was making it up or jumping to conclusions. Maybe they thought I was covering my own mistakes, but I know someone did this. I know they wanted me dead just like they wanted Ben dead.

She nodded.

"What made you change your mind about my fire?"

"I think I might know –"

Before she could take another breath, the door swung open startling us both. I gasped; I heard Steph giggle quietly.

"Happy Birthday!" Cristina cheered.

Birthday? I had been too caught up in everything else to even consider the existence of a birthday. It didn't really mean anything to me, just another trip around the sun, just another 365 days. It was such a random thought that I needed to be celebrated simply for existing. For Cristina to have decided to do anything annoyed me slightly because the way she left me made me think she was never coming back. I'm glad she did though.

Cristina held a small cupcake with a single candle being held by nothing but a mountain of chocolate icing. The flame was lit, my gaze fixed on the burning wick. It danced around with each step. As Cristina came closer the smell of the burning wax grew stronger and stronger. The sound of roaring flames brushed through my ear. I was back. Back in the house. Back in the fire. I could see flames rising up the walls, Cristina stood still, just holding the cake. I moved my legs across the bed until they were handing off the end, I prepared for impact with the floor as I stepped off.

"We have to get out, what are you doing?" I raced out of the room Cristina's hand in mine. It became harder to breath. Dylan stood in the doorway of the main entrance. Reception was full of people, they weren't moving, or rushing. Cristina pulled me back, all I could hear was roaring flames, the fire was getting stronger. I couldn't see it, but the heat was real, and the sounds filled my head.

SPARKS OF BETRAYAL

"Dylan!" I screamed, "why aren't you doing anything?"

He froze.

"Why is no one doing anything." My cries were met with confused expressions, a few concerned. I pulled my hand from Cristina's as my hands began to burn. I took the chance to run, I tried running from the flames, but the heat followed. My eyes dried from the heat on my face, I blinked trying to ease the discomfort. It was hard to breathe, my chest felt as if it was closing in on itself.

That's all I remember; I woke up back in the room. There was no sign of any fire which I thought was impossible, it was there, I felt it.

JUPITER

Chapter 20

Cristina was watching me through the window, that's when I realized, I had moved. The room was completely different. It was plain, even more plain than the other one. I signaled at Cristina to come in, she shook her head.

Why?

Why wasn't she just coming in?

I shot back a confused expression, I couldn't understand. Her expression was sombre as if someone had died.

SPARKS OF BETRAYAL

Was it me? Had I died? Was this it?

The afterlife... I'll be honest this isn't what I expected. It's just like life, but it does feels different. I could still feel the blanket covering my legs and I could still smell the horrible hospital smell, but I couldn't hear anything. I shook the bed with my legs and there was nothing, I tried speaking and I heard none of it.

I frowned at Cristina's face, it was still and unreadable. I couldn't tell what was happening in her head like I usually could. I stared out the window, I couldn't see much of the outside world, only a small square window decorated the white wall. There was no more to this bland room. Suddenly I felt better about the room I had before at least it had some character. Cristina was gone.

What kind of afterlife was this?

I couldn't even see her anymore. *But she can't see me anymore either, yes, my body is still there but not the living version of me right so I could just walk off.*

I tried to move my arms to get myself out of the bed. I was held back by restraints. Why was I held by –

"Meryl." A man walked in. Dylan? *Was he dead too?*

I tried to get myself out of the restraints again, he put his hand on mine... I felt it. I felt his hand. It was soft. He couldn't be dead, there was no way but that would mean I wasn't either.

Why was Cristina so sad? Why did Dylan come in and not Cristina? Did she not want to see me?

"Dylan?" I croaked.

There was no answer. He brushed his hand against mine again and walked away. It was then I finally realised who he was.

"Ben" I gasped. I really had died. I died from a birthday candle. Cristina killed me... I let that sink in for a few seconds before Ben returned.

"You're not dead Meryl. Not quite."

I was confused, if I wasn't dead how come Ben Matthews was standing right in front of me, not only that but he was addressing me by name. He was definitely talking to me, there was no mistaking that.

"Who started the fires?" That was all I could think of surely, he had been watching or had found some sort of answer.

"I know how they were started."

"That's good enough."

Ben stepped closer towards me, lit a match and threw it onto my bed.

Chapter 21

My eyes opened sharply, my heart beating loudly.

"Woah, Meryl. You're okay, it's okay." I heard Cristina's voice. Her hand grabbing hold of mine tightly. My breathing was rapid, was I couldn't make sense of anything I had just seen. "What happened?" She asked softly.

"I saw Ben." I whispered, "I thought it was Dylan at first, but it was definitely Ben."

"He's alive?" She said.

JUPITER

"I don't think so."

"I don't understand"

"Neither do I."

"What exactly happened?"

"I was in a room – a white one. You were sad outside as if I'd died or something and there he was. He walked in told me I wasn't dead, so I was a bit confused –"

"Slow down." Her gentle voice was dreamy.

"I asked who started the fires..."

"What did he say?" She became slightly agitated. "He didn't give a name, but he threw a lit match at me."

"Could have been a hint to what caused it." Steph said, closing the door.

"How long have you been here?" Cristina laughed nervously.

"Not long enough. How are you, Meryl?" She tilted her head. I hated when people did that, it felt like a sign of weakness on my part, as if I'd revealed too much and had them worry.

"There's no need to worry." I smiled.

"It was completely my fault I should have thought."

"No, I shouldn't have been so dramatic, I'm sorry."

SPARKS OF BETRAYAL

"Meryl Evans, don't you dare apologize for your feelings, do you understand me?"

I nodded, I quite liked keeping my vulnerability hidden so I knew that I'd be apologizing for it until the day I die.

"They're letting you come home." Steph smiled.

"Even after yesterday?" Both Cristina and I were shocked at the words.

"Providing you have somewhere safe to stay."

"I don't –"

"You can stay with me." Cristina blurted out, I don't think she thought about what she was saying until afterwards. "Yvette moved out."

"What?"

"She said I wasn't good enough and she'd found somewhere else, she was only still living with me because we'd gotten used to each other's friendly company." Cristina sighed.

"Cristina - You should have said. I'm sorry. It's all my fault." I whined.

"Did you set fire to your house?"

"No."

"Then it's not your fault." Her voice was reassuring and gentle. I didn't deserve it. I didn't deserve her. "You can stay with me until we find you somewhere else."

"Thank you." I whispered.

She smiled. Her smile was my favourite thing, it lit up every room but that's what made her sadness even more devastating.

"When can I leave?" The feelings of dread I had about leaving had disappeared. Now I knew I'd see Cristina every day and I'd have somewhere to stay that wasn't so bland and didn't smell of sanitizer.

"If all is well, tomorrow afternoon," Steph said, her expression was a mix of both happiness and sadness. I sensed that she was happy for me to leave and sad that she wouldn't get to see me every day. I suppose I'm being rather optimistic with the latter. She opened the door; a gust of heat blew inwards. Cristina must have noticed because she grabbed my hand.

"It's just warm air," she whispered. "You're okay."

"I'm okay," I echoed her words. My breathing quickened slightly.

"Say it again," she said closing the door.

"I'm okay." I repeated.

SPARKS OF BETRAYAL

"Do you want me to stay tonight? I don't like the idea of leaving you alone right now."

"Honestly, I'm fine. Do whatever you need to."

"I won't leave just yet."

"Don't let me keep you."

She laughed, "you're not keeping me." She sat on the side of the bed with her hand on mine. My stomach fluttered; I still loved her. Her laugh – Her voice deepened into a giggle. Her laugh always came with a cute smile, even now she was the exact same as she had been the first time, I met her. Her smile was breath-taking. She was breath-taking. I sighed.

"What is it?" She asked, her tone seemed worried.

"Just - You." I whispered.

"Me?" she laughed. There it was again, that smile.

"You're perfect." I whispered, the words escaped my mouth, I didn't even know they were there until it was too late.

"Excuse me?"

"I - I'm sorry."

"No, don't be sorry. It's – " She stuttered, "I should – I should go." She smiled as she stepped out of the room. I shouldn't have said anything.

JUPITER

"What happened?" Steph peeped around the door.

"Do you just watch everything I do?" I joked.

"No, I have things to do," she said. "I just so happened to be looking in your direction when everything seemed to turn awkward."

"No, everything's fine."

"Mhm," Steph nodded.

I understood quickly that there was simply no point in lying. But thankfully she left before I had the chance to say anything else.

Chapter 22

I stayed by myself for much of the rest of the day, I had nothing to do but wait. I was finally allowed out, but now I'd made it awkward with Cristina. If she changes her mind about me moving in with her, I'll have to stay. I can't stay in here any longer despite what I said earlier about not caring anymore. I have nothing to do, my whole life revolved around solving crime I'm nothing without a case file in my hand. Laying here, I'm nothing. I closed my eyes for what I hoped would be the last time stuck within the white walls of the hospital.

JUPITER

Chapter 23

The door squeaked open; the clock ticked past three. The room was dark, and I was alone. Footsteps approached the bed, I was sweating, and I was paralyzed with fear. My breathing slowed until it was almost silent. What if the person who tried to kill me before had come back to finish the job?

"Meryl" they whispered.

"Cristina?" I sat up in shock.

"Yeah" she giggled. "I'm sorry."

SPARKS OF BETRAYAL

"Oh my God, Cristina you can't sneak up on people like that."

"I'm sorry they wouldn't let me in earlier so Steph snuck me in."

"Right, okay."

"I'll sleep on the chair" she said sliding into the armchair placed next to the bed, "sorry for disturbing you."

I smiled as I slid back down into bed. She came back for me. She came back – for me. Even after what I had said.

Chapter 24

"Are you ready to go home?" Cristina asked? I hadn't even been given a minute for my eye to adjust to the light pouring through the window. "I know I didn't take you down to the garden's when I promised I would so how about we start there?" She smiled. She seemed even more excited to be taking me out than I was to be getting out.

I nodded. I still couldn't believe she came back.

"Steph's going to bring your breakfast up in a minute."

"Okay." I couldn't quite believe that I was finally getting out, but what was I supposed to do when I was out?

SPARKS OF BETRAYAL

"You alright?" She tilted her head.

"Yeah, why?"

"You don't seem too excited to leave."

"I am, I promise." I sighed, "I-"

"I got you some toast." Steph said as she opened the door. "You ready to leave?"

"Yeah" I smiled.

"You're going to miss me though, right?"

"Of course, I am."

"I'll be back later to change your dressings for the last time before letting you go. She smiled as she left the room again.

"Sorry, what were you going to say?" Cristina said, I could tell she was trying to return to what we were saying before, but I had thought about it and decided to keep quiet.

"Nothing interesting," I replied.

"I'm sure it was."

Her eyes found mine and silence filled the room. It wasn't awkward, it was comforting. The woman I had spent my whole life chasing was right in front of me, she was really here. Her face was one only associated with movie stars, her skin was young, and her hair was fine.

"You need to eat that for us to go down to the garden."

"I'm not hungry."

"They won't let you leave without eating, something to do with the calories you need for your burns to heal."

"How are they still not healed?"

"They're getting there, the scar tissue's just taking a while." Her voice was so reassuring, I couldn't understand why Yvette would let her go.

"Fine." I took a bite of the toast. It was just like every other piece of toast I'd had while being here, but it was different. Everything was different, even Steph was acting weird. I put it down to me finally leaving but there was definitely something else going on.

"When you've finished that we can go to the gardens. Are you okay to walk there?"

"Yeah, don't worry about me."

"That's my job now" she scoffed. She sounded somewhat sarcastic.

"No, I'm serious. Don't worry about me, I'm fine."

SPARKS OF BETRAYAL

"I'll believe it when I see it." She stood up and began walking around the room, I could tell she was getting impatient with me.

"What's that supposed to mean?"

"Listen, I get you don't like being vulnerable, your career beat that into you, but I am not someone you should be hiding it all from."

I laughed, "where is all of this coming from?"

"I'm just making sure you're okay."

"Well, I am." I smiled. "I've finished the toast too."

She smiled at the empty plate. "I'll take it down to the kitchen, you get yourself ready." As she left the room, I let out a sigh. Could she see through me or was she being friendly?

I looked over at the pile of clothes Cristina had brought in. It was just a hoodie and leggings, but they were freshly washed, unlike these hospital clothes. I changed into the new clothes and sat on the edge of the bed. I put my trainers on and brushed my hands through my hair.

"You ready?" Cristina said cheerfully as she re-entered the room.

"Yeah" I whispered.

We made our way through the corridor to the lift at the end, it took us down to the ground floor. The crisp winter air burnt my chest as I inhaled the beautiful scent of the flowers. Most of them had died but the smell still lingered. "There aren't many flowers out this time of year but at least the sun is shining." I could hear the smile in Cristina's voice. The sun was in fact shining but the grass was still damp from the few days of rain we had just endured.

"My mother always said you can never appreciate the true beauty of the sun until you've been through a storm." Cristina's voice was soft, that's how I knew her eyes had faded into a state of reminiscence.

"It was hardly a storm," I laughed.

"No, I know but this garden just reminded me of her."

"Cute" I smiled, I wasn't entirely sure how to react, I turned to see beads of tears streaming down her scarlet cheeks.

"Woah, I'm sorry."

She brushed the tears away, embarrassed. "Sorry, ignore that." She laughed.

"No, what is it?"

"Nothing." She turned to the bush and ran her hand over the flower petals.

SPARKS OF BETRAYAL

"It's clearly something."

"Nothing important." I tilted my head; I hated when other people did it, but I couldn't help it. "You can go ahead I'll catch you up." She said.

I stepped towards the water fountain, it was the centre piece of the garden, full of coins and hopeful wishes. I turned to look up at the building I had finally escaped knowing some would never be free. My mind wandered back to Ben. I was lucky, I'm alive.

"I wished for you when you first came in." Cristina whispered as she walked up behind me.

"Thank you." my voice broke, there was no hiding the emotion in those words. She put her arms around me, pulling me into a tight hug. It had been years since anyone had hugged me, I held on tight in fear of letting go. I couldn't let her go.

"If we go back up, we can get your dressings changed and go home." Cristina said.

"We've only just got down here, can we stay a while."

She nodded. I was like a child asking permission to stay longer in the park. I walked around the rest of the garden, there wasn't much which was expected for the time of year, but I acted interested in every leaf, I didn't want to go back inside, I liked the way the fresh air burnt, and I loved how the sunlight splashed along the dew coated leaves.

"There's more around the corner," Cristina laughed. "You don't have to linger around that one bush."

I wasn't aware I was making it that obvious, "I just love these leaves."

"Meryl, I won't make you go back inside until you're ready." I smiled, how did she know that's exactly what I was thinking?

I took a few more minutes to look around and take in what I'd missed from the outside world.

"I'm ready."

"Are you sure?" If I could stay outside forever I would but I couldn't wait to get discharged.

We made our way back to the room. I began packing the few things I had left. I slipped the bracelet into my trainer and sat awaiting Steph and Cristina.

After a lengthy wait Cristina burst through the door, "Steph's gone."

"What do you mean?"

"She's gone, it's not the end of the world I have someone else."

"What do you mean she's gone though?"

SPARKS OF BETRAYAL

"I suppose she's gone home."

I agreed silently, I couldn't understand why she had left right before I was due to be discharged. Another woman came to show Cristina how to change the dressings, she knew how to do it already, but I wasn't allowed to go until she was shown. The woman was silent, she just simply showed Cristina what to do and left. Once she had left, she signed the paper for us to leave and walked away.

"She was strange." Cristina said, "we're free to go."

I couldn't help but wonder where Steph had gone, she hadn't said a word to us since breakfast. I didn't mean to worry but what else was I to do?

Before leaving I took one last glance at the table, the table that so much evidence had been upon. I imagined the file sitting there, I regret closing it again but there was nothing more I could do. I went over and over the evidence again and again on the way to Cristina's flat, but it was the same as it had always been. Nothing more, nothing less.

Chapter 25

I sat alone in the flat. There was nothing more to do, I settled on the fact that my final case will never be solved. I was overwhelmed by the guilt of dragging it all backup, why would I do that... I should know better than anyone that sometimes you've got to accept the answers. The Ben Matthews case was the first case I failed to solve, even though they made their decision I was still unconvinced. There was just no way he had done it... There was only so much I could have done to change their mind and by now I saw it best to leave it as it was, I couldn't bear to see anyone else getting hurt.

SPARKS OF BETRAYAL

I stared at the wall, my mind wondered back to that day, the day of my fire. Still no cause, just as there hadn't been for Ben. I suppose no one truly understands how it felt to be told your accident was brushed off as suicide, which is why I thought that the same bitch set fire to both my house and Ben's... The only problem here was... we didn't know who, we ran out of suspects there was no more evidence, that was it. It was all over. Ben never got justice.

I looked down at my legs, I ran my finger along the scars. I survived... Ben didn't. What if that had been me? My finger continues following the scars. Cristina stepped through the door.

"Hey, you alright?" She looked down at my leg.

"Yeah," I smiled, I lied.

"I've made lasagna for dinner." She exclaimed, she opened the oven to reveal an uncooked lasagna, "If I put it on now it'll be done by five. We could watch something?"

"Sure." I've no idea where she found the time to make a whole lasagna from scratch.

"I'll set the timer for an hour." She turned on the oven and set the timer, I couldn't take my eyes off of her and I couldn't believe my luck. How had a girl like me gotten a girl like her? Well, I hadn't really, she didn't like me like that I was simply living in her flat, but that was enough for me.

"I'll put something on in there," I nodded towards the living room.

"Choose whatever you like." I didn't put much thought into choosing I turned the TV on and left it on that same channel, I was hoping we would talk enough that whatever was on in the background wouldn't matter.

"Good choice," Cristina cheered. I sat on the chair while she sat on the furthest end of the sofa. I kept running my finger along the scars on my arms, in this flat was the only place I could feel comfortable without covering them up. Only in front of Cristina.

"They're beautiful," she said looking down at them. We must have been looking at different things because all I saw were ugly marks along my skin. It wasn't me.

"You don't have to lie to make me feel better you know."

"I'm not lying I really do think they're beautiful."

"I've had it though, haven't I? In the context of love."

"What do you mean?"

"Cristina, I'm fifty-six. I spent my whole life so dedicated to work; I didn't even give myself a chance at anything else."

SPARKS OF BETRAYAL

"It's not too late though," she shuffled closer to me.

I kept my eyes on my scars, "no one's going to love this." I scoffed.

"I do." I knew she was only saying it to make me feel better, she didn't mean it. "You're beautiful."

"No, I'm not."

"Meryl Evans," she put her hand beneath my chin and lifted it up, "you are gorgeous."

"Okay," I scoffed.

"I'm telling the truth."

I smiled at her; tears began welling up in my eyes. I was embarrassed, I didn't want her to have to watch me be anything other than a strong detective, but I couldn't hold it in any longer.

"It's okay," she said pulling me into another hug. I buried my head in her shoulder and cried, I just cried. I hadn't released such emotion in front of anyone before, I kept it all very well hidden, but I couldn't hide anymore, not from Cristina.

"Sorry," I whispered.

"No need to apologize, it's what I'm here for." I smiled. Cristina ran her finger along the scars on my cheeks. As I pulled away, she sat back on the sofa to watch the tv. I couldn't take my eyes off her. I still loved her, but she doesn't deserve a monster like me. I brushed my hands over my scars. Time flew as we sat together, and the smell of Cristina's lasagne came creeping into the room. I smiled; Cristina must have noticed.

"This'll make you feel better," she said as she lifted herself off the sofa. Once she left the room, I took the opportunity to look around the room. I thought it'd be rude to judge it while she was inside not only that, but it was my nature to look around for clues. I wasn't searching for anything in particular, but anything would do. Nothing stood out, to begin with, except for the small folder shoved under the chest of drawers. There was no time to investigate before Cristina returned with two plates of freshly cooked lasagne.

"Here you are," she gleamed, handing me one of the plates. "Careful it's hot." I grabbed a cushion from the sofa and propped it on my lap I put the plate on top. "Garlic bread is probably burnt, I'm sorry."

"It's okay." I laughed; she had never been an amazing cook she was just too bad at multi-tasking so who knows how she managed a lasagne.

Now I had noticed the folder it's all I could think about. I knew it was there, and I know it's rude to go rummaging through people's personal belongings, but it just looked too suspicious I mean who hides a folder under a chest of drawers unless it was full of something suspicious? All I had to do was wait for her to go to bed, that was the only chance I had.

"Here it is," she placed the garlic bread on the coffee table each slice cut very evenly. "You can have my room, I'll sleep in here."

Fucking typical.

"No, it's fine I sleep better on the sofa anyway."

"No, no I insist."

"Honestly the sofa is so much better."

"Are you sure? You're free to sleep in the bed for a few nights."

"Positive." I nodded. Sleep was out of the question for tonight anyway and it's a good job too because I'd never get to sleep on the sofa.

"Okay, it's just in that room down the hall if you need anything through the night, and I mean anything, anytime."

We sat for a while; the time ticked by slowly. I didn't know what to say, my brain was full of different scenario's surrounding the file. It was just lying there it must have been so full of interesting facts for it to be hidden the way it was.

JUPITER

"I'm getting pretty tired and it's quite late, are you ready to go to bed?" Cristina asked, I didn't know what to say, it wasn't my house.

"Do you want me to wash up? I'll be up for a while anyway."

"No, of course not, leave it there I'll sort it in the morning." She said, "do you need a new dressing?"

"I don't think I really need them anymore."

"Maybe you should, just for tonight at least." She tilted her head as she usually did.

"Fine." I said, I hated the itchiness of the bandages, but I suppose an infection would be inconvenient right now besides, I don't know anything about that sofa.

"I'll be back with your pillows and stuff, I'm sorry tonight's been so boring."

"Don't worry at all." I replied, "it was actually really nice for once."

A smile spread across her face before she left for the bedding I probably wouldn't need. I placed my plate on top of hers and took them both to the kitchen. I placed the dishes in the bottom of the sink and grabbed a glass from the draining board. I thought it'd be better to get myself the glass of water that I usually need about three o clock now to avoid making noise later. I placed the

SPARKS OF BETRAYAL

glass on the side as Cristina passed holding a mountain of blankets, I couldn't help but laugh. I wasn't even sure she could see where she was going. Clearly, she couldn't as she crashed into the living room door frame. She fell to the ground, the mountain of bedding falling on top of her, she was silent for a few seconds before erupting into fits of laughter. I couldn't control my laughter we were both helpless, gasping for air between giggles. There it was again... her laughter. I'd do anything to keep it with me forever. I'd keep it like some sort of fairy dust and hang it round my neck, so I'd never be parted from the beautiful sound ever again.

Chapter 26

Cristina had been in bed for hours, surely, she was asleep by now. I shuffled over to the file sliding it out from under the chest of drawers and opened it.

I gasped.

It was my file, not only that but it was combined with the Ben Matthews case file. It was too good to be true there's no way I just so happened to stumble upon these two specific files. What were they doing in Cristina's house? I get that she took them away from me but surely, she took them back to the lockers? I rummaged

SPARKS OF BETRAYAL

nevertheless; nothing was new. Of course, nothing was new Cristina would have mentioned it if there was anything.

I put the file back where I found it, I trusted there was nothing new and I wasn't ready to look through pictures of my house as a pile of ash. But why the file was hidden in her house was something I needed to find out. I couldn't ask her that'd just be exposing myself as a sneak. She didn't have to offer me a place here and if she found out what I had just found I don't think she'd want me here anymore and I really needed to stay here.

'Well tonight was anti-climactic' I thought. I had spent al night so excited to unveil the secrets hiding in the file and there was nothing, nothing at all.

I picked the bracelet out of my shoe and ran it along the back of my hand, just as I had the first day it was given to me. My father gave it to me the day my mother died, it was her favourite bracelet she never took it off. They were going to bury it with her until my father decided he wanted me to have it. I wish he had let her go with it I feared losing it and when I did the guilt was strong, it followed me everywhere. There wasn't a day that passed where I didn't think of the whereabouts of this bracelet. I never spoke about my mother at work, I suppose that's why they gave me her murder case. There were two suspects and within a week, one of those were dead so that narrowed it down quite a bit. My father then served life in prison for both murders.

I was never quite sure why he did it, the only explanation we scraped together was that he was upset with how much time she was spending with me. It was my fault, I blamed myself every day, I'll never know the truth, but that answer satisfied me. I blamed myself and I will until the end of time.

I never told anyone explicitly, but they found out, I was forced into compassionate leave for a month completely against my will, I couldn't believe it. In hindsight it was one of the best things for me but at the time I just wanted to work, staying home doing nothing made me feel lazy, people needed cases solved and I was out of action. It wasn't that I thought no one else could solve them it was that no one could solve them like me. My brain seemed to be wired specifically to solve crime, I solved three cases in the time it took the others to solve one and I wasn't doing half a job I was working hard, I solved every case, not one stone was left unturned, everyone got their answers. My reputation grew so good that people from all over the world were contacting me to solve their murder cases but not only those it was all cases, missing people, murder, and even lost items and I was successful every time. Until now. Ben was the exception. My magic had worn off and it crushed me. Not only was I never going to be able to solve another case, but I also wasn't even going to be given one.

Retirement's a bitch. I only agreed to retire if I was given the Ben Matthews case. It took months to even find a lead, it was a difficult case. A fire with no cause. Some may say impossible.

"How long have you been up?"

"I've only just woken up," I lied. I looked over to the clock that ticked on the wall, 5:42am. I gasped; I'd been thinking all night.

"That's why the blankets haven't moved," she laughed. "Listen, I have something to tell you." She sounded serious, it was that voice people put on when they're about to tell you some unbelievably bad news like someone died.

"Who died?" She was taken aback by my instant tone recognition.

"Steph." She whispered.

"Steph?" I repeated, "no, you're wrong."

"I'm sorry."

I didn't know her that well I'd only actually known her the time I was in the hospital. I had seen her around when we used to bring people in but nothing more.

JUPITER

"How?" I suppose the detective in me was taking over again.

"Suicide."

"Didn't see that coming."

"Most often you don't y'know. In my experience, it's the happiest people." She didn't take her eyes off the floor.

"When?" I was asking questions on top of question trying to make sense of the situation.

"I assume when we were in the gardens, she was found in the on-call room in the hospital."

"Why?" That was the stupidest question of them all, no one really knows why people take their own lives, if people knew why the mental health services would be better funded. If we knew she was going ot do something like that we'd have done everything to talk her out of it. I think maybe that's why many people stay quiet, they don't want to be talked out of anything, their mind is already made up. None of that makes it any easier for those left behind.

She shrugged; I'd be more concerned if she knew why Steph did it because that meant there was time to help. "She was a nurse; she's seen so many things. It's not an easy job maybe the pressure got the better of her?"

"She loved her job."

SPARKS OF BETRAYAL

"Maybe she did when she was in the room with you but how would you know anything outside of that room?"

I shook my head.

"If I had to guess I'd say she was waiting until you were leaving."

"Stop," I whispered. It infuriated me that she was trying to make sense of a situation she obviously knew nothing about. For me to know what happened I would have to get back in touch with the police force, this would be way harder than I initially thought though because all the people I grew up with, everyone in my unit had the decency to have a happy retirement, they've all put their detective years behind them, I don't think I ever will.

Chapter 27

I stared blankly into the distance for most of the day, I didn't know what I was looking at it was mostly blurry, I had no right to be upset and I appreciated that, it was her family I felt sorry for. I doubt there was any warning for them either, not only them but whoever found her depending on how she went, it wouldn't have been nice to see.

Cristina had gone out to the shop, but she had been there for a while unless she hadn't been, and time was going slower than usual. There was nothing much to do other than feel sorry for people. I wasn't even sure I was

SPARKS OF BETRAYAL

going to be invited to the funeral I mean why should I? I'd known her a month.

It took longer than I thought for the realization to dawn on me; she gave me the bracelet; she knew where she found it. Was she there at the fire? For her to have that exact bracelet she would have had to find it around my house, but I couldn't even find it around my house. It had been years since I saw it, and she knew it was mine because she gave it to me.

I had to stop thinking about it, I could keep going deeper for hours but it wouldn't help anyone. I needed to get out, go for a walk somewhere. I couldn't take being stuck inside anymore.

The lights flickered as I rummaged through her wardrobe in search of something that would completely cover me. I settled in joggers and a hoodie that didn't draw too much attention to myself. I left the building having locked the door behind me.

My legs moved me forwards, but I didn't know where I was going. I just kept moving, it was as if I was trying to walk away from everything but no matter how far I walked it'd follow me. I made my way to a sheltered bench and watched the people pass.

They walked. Each person passed, facing forwards. The sound of crashing waves played as the soundtrack to their journeys. Each face concealed a different story to the face in front, the face behind, and to the face who walked lovingly beside them. The sun shone bright on frowning faces and even brighter on those with beaming smiles. Each story was different, however, in some peculiar way, in that moment each story, writing, living, experiencing the same next line... they walked.

The loose rocks shuffled beneath their shoes, scraping the concrete floor. Coats rustled as the people rummaged through their pockets searching for something. No one knows what until the object is released into the open air.

Rocks, tissues, coins...

A young boy and his grandfather walked by slowly, they smiled at the crashing waves. The oldest of the two reached into his deep pocket withdrawing a shiny coin. His hand travelled to his grandson's hand, he smiled, Everette watched as the boys lips moved to the rhythm of 'Thank you.'

Their voices mumbled engaging conversations so little people would hear. They turn to laugh with the person walking by their side. Hand in hand, couples young and old walked down the never-ending path. Lone people strutted past silently. The strangers passing by may mean nothing to each other, but they mean everything to someone. Someone who many people will miss the opportunity to meet.

SPARKS OF BETRAYAL

A handful of people stop to admire the bright blue sea sparkling in the sunlight. The few who's eyes dared look beyond the dark green hue of the horizon shuddered. As they stand, they think. Their thoughts are not there to be heard by the likes of Everette but there to stay in the minds of those who think them. He can guess but he'll never truly know.

A man stumbles to the bench, his hair curly and free. He rested his wooden cane by his side and took out a photograph from his pocket.

A beautiful, young girl on a swing in the middle of a woodland. Her long, curly auburn hair looked perfectly placed with a flower headband keeping it out of her face. Sunlight gleamed on her perfect skin. She smiled at the camera with glistening blue eyes. Everette stared in awe. The man looked down and sighed. He looked out at the sea, his thoughts trapped inside his head. His hand shook as he lifted the picture levelling it on the horizon.

I stepped away and continued walking down the seafront, as I looked out to sea, I noticed the starlings. A murmuration of Starlings filled the sky, they flew rhythmically finding themselves gathering in different formations with the sunset as a beautiful backdrop. They almost looked like shadows as they danced around the sky. I paused to admire their routine.

"There you are!" Dylan said breathlessly, "Cristina's going mad in there trying to find you."

"She went shopping."

"Meryl, you've been gone for hours."

"I can't have been," I laughed looking up as the moon emerging from the clouds. Time was flying by and all I could do was watch the night close in.

"We need to go home." Dylan said pulling me away from the railing. We made our way back to Cristina's house.

***

"There you are," Cristina gleamed as I stepped in through the front door, Dylan close behind me. "You had me worried for a while."

"Should you tell her, or should I?" Dylan asked.

"Tell me what?"

"I'm going away for a few days, I don't know whether it's safe for you to stay here alone, I thought you could stay with Dylan just until Friday." I stared at the calendar; it was only Tuesday.

"You don't trust me?"

"Of course, I do but I just think you need someone for now."

SPARKS OF BETRAYAL

"Okay." I reluctantly agreed to stay with Dylan. His voice was dreamy but that's about all I knew about him. I didn't trust him after the lies he told before, but I didn't want to worry Cristina while she was away. I never asked where she was going, not because I didn't care I just didn't want her to think she needed to tell me, which sounds ridiculous now because I really do want to know where she went. I wanted to know why she had dumped me with Dylan knowing what he had done in the past. It wouldn't have surprised me at all to find out he was behind the fire's if I'm being completely honest. He didn't give anything away.

I gazed back at Cristina whose face seemed to have relaxed since I agreed to stay with him.

"Do you want me gone tonight?"

"Tomorrow morning."

I felt like such a burden. The way they had to decide where to put me, why couldn't I just fend for myself like I had most of my life anyway? Why did my house have to be the one to burn down? Why couldn't I have been the one to die? Not Ben. He had a family, people who cared. People who even now, twenty years later are still heart broken. It'd be so much easier on Cristina, she wouldn't have to worry about anything and without a doubt she'd have forgotten about it within a month, why couldn't it all have gone like that? But it didn't, and now we're here.

Still with no answers. I failed the one thing I thought I was good at. How pathetic was I becoming? I didn't want anyone to see me failing everyone like that. I needed to get away, hide from everything.

"Okay," I agreed. "Only until Friday." I began to grow sceptical of where she was going, she promised she wouldn't leave and then two days after I leave the hospital she leaves. I don't need to know everything she does in her life, but this was strange. What was worse was that I hadn't even seen Dylan for weeks and there was no trust between us. Nothing made sense but it was only two nights, what was I supposed to do?

"Thank you for finding her." Cristina turned to Dylan, the sudden change in attitude toward him worried me. We hadn't even determined his innocence in the Ben Matthews case, I couldn't trust him.

SPARKS OF BETRAYAL

What if it was a trick?

What if he was behind the fires?

What if he was going to try and get me again?

Was Cristina behind this?

Did they both want me dead?

Why?

What did I ever do to them?

I thought I could trust Cristina...

I can't trust her.

I can't trust her.

I can't trust anyone.

JUPITER

Chapter 28

4th December 2020.

I'm sat in Dylan's car looking up at a worn-down house, if I had to guess he was going it set it alight for insurance it looks like he needs a new place. I'm writing in case I'm inside when it goes up in flames. He was acting weird in Cristina's house, and I can't understand why she's started trusting him again. I suppose I must have missed a lot while I was in the hospital, but I'd never trust him, especially since his

SPARKS OF BETRAYAL

innocence is yet to be proven. The house really is falling apart, the roof lifts in the wind, dust falls off the door when you open and close it, it's horrible. It's made of stone, so I assume it's quite old.

It's made of stone.

Sure, inside would be scorched but the building itself will still be standing, more than just a pile of ash. More than just dust. Dylan's shouting at me now to go inside, I guess I'll envelope this and hide it in the car.

If you are reading this and that house is nothing but stone walls and ash, you know what happened and you know who's to blame.

I placed the enveloped letter in between the back seats, I made sure none of it could be seen before leaving the car. The last thing I needed was Dylan finding it. I shut the door firmly and walked slowly to the front door. He's still waiting in the doorway, his body pressed against the wall. I could tell he was getting angry at me. As I approached him, he sighed.

"What took you so long?" I assumed he didn't see me writing.

"You couldn't see?"

"The windows are tainted, so obviously not."

"Oh, okay," I sighed with relief. Why hadn't I been more careful, what if he could see? What was I thinking? I'm a detective for fuck's sake you'd think I'd be better at things like this. I'm not sly or cunning, I don't commit the crime or defend the suspects, I don't lie or deceive, I solve.

He led me into the kitchen where he pulled out a chair for me to sit, the kitchen itself was nice, modern, not long been upgraded. The whole room was grey, ash grey tiles lined the walls behind the oven and the fridge which transitioned into a dark grey the higher up it went. The floor was cold stone, every step echoed. The chair was made up of a solid grey cushion in a painted oak frame painted as grey as the rest of the room. The clock was a grey washed white

"Why is everything so grey?" I asked.

"It's nice, no?" He replied.

I took one last look around before answering, "I guess I've seen worse."

"Of course you have, with your line of work, your reputation and years in the job I suppose you've seen it all." I couldn't tell if he was being sarcastic, but I shot him a dirty look as soon as his back turned. "Are you hungry?"

SPARKS OF BETRAYAL

"A little I guess."

"Perfect, so am I." He turned to the fridge and took out a cold pizza. The fridge looked practically empty, something I'd expect to see if he was about to burn it down. "I can heat it up if you like."

"It's better cold." The pizza had been prepared prior to my arrival, it had already been cooked, it had already been taken out of the box. If he wanted me dead there's a chance he'd tamper with the pizza. I waited for him to take a bite before I even considered trying it. As he did, I was still sceptical, what was I supposed to think? I didn't want to be here. I didn't feel safe.

I took the smallest slice from the plate to avoid concern.

"Cristina says you have to eat for your burns to heal."

"They're fine, they're just scars. I showed him my arms."

"I'm talking about the ones on your legs"

Of course you are.

I watched everything Dylan did, every time he tapped his fingers on the chair, every time he rustled his hair, I watched everything. Just in case. Just in case he was to do whatever it was I thought he was planning. If I'm completely honest, I don't know what I think he's going to do. All I knew was there was an unsolved murder case and as far as I'm concerned it has Dylan Jones written all over it. Perhaps I was getting carried away, or maybe I was so desperate for answers I was pointing the finger at anyone who could have been anywhere near at the time but that's not the case, I know me, I do. I know that I would never confront someone without any evidence. There is evidence, there's something about him that makes me feel uneasy and my impressions of people are usually right.

Anyway, I'm getting carried away in my thoughts again...

By now Dylan had separated the pizza onto two plates, I noticed that my plate was significantly fuller than his. "Dylan, I'm not going to eat all of that."

"You have to, Cristina's orders."

"I don't see Cristina around, do you?" I said, pushing the plate back.

"You're going to eat it," his anger was building, and in the situation, I was in I didn't want to make it worse.

"What if I don't?" I asked, I couldn't help the temptation.

"You really want to know?"

I nodded.

"Just wait..."

That to me was a clear indication that he was planning something. I was trapped, playing by his rules. Nothing

SPARKS OF BETRAYAL

in these past few days were making sense, maybe it would have been easier for me to stay in hospital, maybe I could have stayed with Steph.

Steph... Did they hear anything else? I grabbed my phone from the table, Dylan grabbed my wrist.

"No phone until you've eaten."

Who the fuck does this man think he is?

I pulled away sharply, putting my phone in my back pocket. I'm sure every woman would just tell me to eat the pizza but then he wins doesn't he. He wins. Maybe playing by his rules would work in my favour in the long run though, but I can't have him thinking he has control over me.

I pulled the plate towards me and began eating, it was just food. No reason to argue over food.

"Good girl."

Ew, don't call me that.

Maybe a log of those letters wouldn't be a bad idea hidden around the outside of the house, in plant pots etc, at least then if anything happens the evidence piles up against him.

It took me half an hour to get through the plate, there wasn't much but the agony of knowing he was already two steps ahead of me put me off the taste.

JUPITER

"I've got to grab something from the car, you can do whatever."

As if I trust you, I thought. He was leaving the building, the perfect time to set this place alight. I watched him through the window, I watched his every step. He really did go to the car; I didn't expect him to. Unless he was getting his supplies.

Stop it!

I needed to stop thinking of the worst-case scenario, it was only two nights.

He walked back towards the house with a box. It was varnished wood with a metal hook to close it. The box was one you'd see perfect women in perfect dresses put pretty written letters in by the river in spring but in his hands, it looked sad and suspicious. He stomped through the door. His boots were heavy, his footsteps echoed through the house.

"I'm going to my room if that's okay."

"Yeah, whatever." He said.

I walked to the room and opened the door. The room was old, I doubt anyone had even looked at it in about twenty years. Dust coated the bedding, the walls, and the wardrobe. I couldn't tell if it was grey or just enveloped in dust. The longer I stayed in the house the more uncomfortable I became. I took my phone out and

SPARKS OF BETRAYAL

started taking photos, no one would have ever believed me had I not collected evidence. I sent the photos to Cristina, had she known where she had sent me, I doubt she'd have let me come.

I noticed a black file within the dust, exactly the same as the one I found in Cristina's house. At this point I wanted to wake up, I wanted it all to have been a nightmare. I've had enough of all of this, nothing's making any sense.

JUPITER

Chapter 29

Cristina took me home. I couldn't stay there, not with him. I never want to see him ever again.

I kept the file. To compare it to the one in Cristina's house. They look the same, the first few pages are exactly the same, but the back pages prove things I never thought I'd see in writing. I was right... it wasn't an accident, none of it was.

There was a match taped onto a piece of card, a match. It hadn't seen a flame; it was a perfect match. Written underneath the match was the words;

Murder Weapon.

SPARKS OF BETRAYAL

"Murder weapon?" I whispered. "An untouched match?"

"It was a lit match." Cristina said, I slammed the folder shut, but it was too late she had already seen it.

"How do you know?"

"Dylan –"

"Dylan!?" I exclaimed.

"Let me finish, the only explanation he could find was a match." She sighed, "so he put one in just in case."

Something stopped me believing her but there was no way I was going anywhere near Dylan again.

He did it, I just have to prove it.

Cristina was leaning against the door frame as I turned around.

"Cristina, I'm a detective not an idiot. I know he did it."

A slight smile spread across her face. "You just can't keep away from it can you?"

"I'm sorry."

"You have nothing to apologize for."

We smiled, my eyes locked with hers.

"Do you want to go out for dinner?" She tilted her head again, "I think you need it."

JUPITER

"Sure," I nodded.

"I'll just get my coat."

***

The restaurant was busy for a Wednesday night, the only table available was in the far corner. We weaved between tables to the corner where we sat under an unlit chandelier. The waitress brought us menus and Cristina began scanning the options. I looked around the room, it was a dark candle-lit restaurant, and the tables were dark brown. There were welcoming flowers on each of the tables I suppose to add colour to the dreary-looking seating area. The carpet was a deep purple, with golden patterns. The whole room looked as if they had tried to have a fancy-looking dining hall and had given up. The most light came from the hole in the wall where the kitchen was.

"Sorry I didn't realise there were candles." Cristina whispered, holding my hand.

"It's okay" I took a breath before smiling at her.

"Can I get any drinks for you?"

"Can I get a pink lemonade please," Cristin smiled.

"Can I have the dragon fruit mocktail, please."

"Of course." She stepped away from the table to make the drinks.

SPARKS OF BETRAYAL

"I didn't have you down as a dragon fruit girl."

"I so had you down as a pink lemonade girl." I laughed, "I bet you'll have the chicken strips with salad."

"You're too good!" She laughed, "you're going to have the macaroni cheese."

"I am!" I cheered. I wasn't going to; I was thinking of the small burger, but I wanted Cristina to feel like she had guessed.

The smile on her face was worth missing out on a burger.

The waitress returned with our drinks, both matching pinks. We ordered the food expecting to have to wait about an hour due to the demand, but we were wrong, within twenty minutes we were sitting with our food in front of us.

"I have a question," Cristina said, leaning towards me.

"You do?" I replied, "what is it?"

"I don't want it to ruin anything though."

I knew exactly what she was going to say. The answer was yes, it'll always be yes. I waited for her to ask the question before getting excited.

"I just wanted to give you a chance."

"A chance?"

"I know you haven't had a chance to be in a relationship because of work and such –"

"Yes. I say yes." I couldn't help myself, I had to let her know.

"Really?" She seemed surprised.

"Of course."

"So, it's official!"

"It is!"

She sounded almost as happy as I felt. All my life I had waited for her. What's better is that she was the one to ask. It was a mutual feeling.

"I love you, Meryl." She gleamed.

"I love you too, Cristina."

We must have been too caught up in the moment to realize the whole police unit frantically searching the restaurant. I nodded towards them; Cristina turned around.

What a way to ruin the moment.

"Is Cristina Faye here?"

"Why are the police looking for you?"

"There's a Cristina over there," the front of house called out.

SPARKS OF BETRAYAL

"I can explain," she pleaded.

What the fuck is going on?

"What have you done?"

"I promise I can explain."

"Cristina, I am arresting you on suspicion of the murder of Ben Matthews and the attempted murder of Meryl Evans. You have the right to remain silent. Anything you say can and will be used against you in a court of law."

"Cristina!" I sat in shock. What was I supposed to say? The murderer I was trying to find was right in front of me the whole time. I trusted her, I was prepared to spend the rest of my life with her.

She burned my house down and invited me to stay because she felt bad, and she asked me out so I wouldn't suspect her. She knew what she was doing, and I fell for it.

I fell for her.

The rest of the restaurant stared at me. They were staring at me because of Cristina but I couldn't help feeling that they couldn't take their eyes off my ugly scars. I covered my face, grabbed my things, and left the table.

I couldn't breathe as I stepped outside into the cold winter air.

JUPITER

Cristina Faye... the problem was I had met her... now I don't know how to live without her. I remembered as I whispered her name in the flames, the flames ignited by sparks of a match. I didn't realize those sparks were the result of betrayal.

SPARKS OF BETRAYAL

Part Two
(Cristina)

SPARKS OF BETRAYAL

JUPITER

To Meryl,

I want to start by saying I didn't want any of this. It's not my fault but at the same time, it's all my fault. I know you're angry at me but please don't end this lifelong friendship before hearing the full story. I love you Meryl and I can't bear the thought of never seeing you again, I know I've messed up, maybe I should have told you but then how was I to know how you would react? I hate myself for what I've done, please come and see me so I can at least explain.

Cristina. XXX

SPARKS OF BETRAYAL

JUPITER

Chapter 1

The police dragged me to the car, I didn't resist because I've seen what happens when people do. They were rough, they made themselves look weak by trying so hard. I sat in the car and said nothing, I knew the tricks the police use to get you to talk, I couldn't afford to say anything now.

I watched the rolling fields pass the window as my mind filled with questions.

How did they even find out?

SPARKS OF BETRAYAL

Who found out? If Meryl couldn't crack the case, I was certain no one else could. I thought I had everything under control.

Evidently, I don't. I'm sat here in a police car on my way to a cell, to stay alone, forever. I'm not saying I don't deserve it of course I do but I thought I'd gotten away with it for 20 years, I'm fifty-seven years old... I should not be on my way to prison.

The one question that overwhelmed my mind the most was; *why?*

There must have been a reason.

People do not kill for nothing; they don't just set fire to people's houses for no reason.

I didn't, I know I didn't.

But why then?

Why did I do it?

I've known Meryl most of my life, we started cadets together. I've envied her career; I've always admired how she worked. She never gave away her secrets and I think that's what made her the best. She never told anyone how, she just got on with it. She never used her reputation against anything, sure she got a lot of jobs out of her ability to solve but she never threw it in any of our faces she simply got on with the job. She was fantastic. She never left a stone unturned, and she made sure everyone had their happy ever after. She made people happy... She made me happy.

So, what made me do it?

As far as I'm concerned, she was the love of my life, so why? Why did I set her house alight? Not only did I wait for her to be inside, I locked the door. I did everything I could to make her die. I suppose it was because I didn't want her to know what I had done to Ben Matthews, and I knew she was the only detective to be able to solve it, so I guess my instinct was to get rid of her.

But why?

The frustration kept building with each mile that passed. I was frustrated with myself but also frustrated because I knew I was going down for something I didn't want to do. I didn't do it alone; in fact, it wasn't even me who lit the match. I wasn't even aware there was a match.

He lied to me.

Chapter 2

I sat in the interrogation room; I had only ever been on the other side of the table so being questioned was new to me. My legs were shaking with anxiety. I could hear my heart racing, what was I supposed to say?

The truth.

I couldn't tell the truth, I wouldn't be able to, he would just deny it all and who are they going to believe?

The woman? I laughed to myself.

The room was blank, with white walls, a grey door and a table in the middle. The chairs on either side were old and grey, everything about the room was bleak and depressing. There wasn't much around to distract you from the questions.

The best thing I could do for myself was to tell the truth, that's what I should do. I'm safe in here, from him I mean. I could tell them the truth and he'll never know. I shook my hair out of my face prepared to tell them everything, every detail. I lifted my head to look at the door, as if by magic the officer walked in; I recognized him immediately.

What?

Dylan stood over me intimidatingly, "don't say a word." He whispered. My heartbeat was the only thing I could hear at that moment and I'm sure he could hear it too. I'm sure he found pleasure in frightening me, but I wasn't going to be silenced by him, he's done enough. I nodded so that he would leave me alone, I thought that'd be enough until I noticed him going to take a seat on the opposite end of the table. He was my interviewer... I was stuck, back at square one. I had absolutely everything against me, I sighed.

"Cristina, she was onto me." He pulled out a stack of handwritten notes, the handwriting was unmistakable. "They were in my car, no wonder she was trying to get out." He slid the notes across to me, I read through them quickly.

SPARKS OF BETRAYAL

"She was suspicious of you, not me." I said, I folded them up and kept them tucked tightly in my hand, it was all I had left of her. "Why am I here, Dylan?"

"You're not innocent, you know that."

"But who found out? Who told them?"

"I did." He said, he didn't say it with shame, he was proud of what he'd done. I suppose he'd do anything to get out of a life sentence.

"Why?" I pleaded, "I did nothing wrong. You lied to me."

"You still did it though Cristina, you were there, you collected the evidence, that was all you."

"I didn't know what we were doing."

"That's on you."

He was getting closer and closer to victory; I was about to be locked up for the rest of my life and all because of him.

"I saw your cute little message to Meryl; I was going to let you go but now I just don't think I can trust you."

I stood up in a rage, I couldn't decide whether to punch him or the wall. I didn't need an assault charge on top of murder and attempted murder, so I aimed for the wall.

"Cristina!" Dylan shouted at me; I stared down at the blood dripping from my knuckles, I held it with my other hand and backed into the corner of the room. "GET AWAY FROM ME!" I screamed; two more officers came running into the room. One came towards me while the other dragged Dylan out of the room. "What happened?" She asked.

The words were stuck, I was overwhelmed by the emotion my eyes welled with tears, I buried my head in her shoulder and cried. My hand was in agony, but I did my best to ignore it.

***

I sat in the hospital waiting room with the officer, it wasn't too busy so I wouldn't be there for long. I was hoping it would be busier so I could get a story together, the truth, I'd have to remember the order, every little detail. My hand distracted me from most of my thoughts.

"Can I request something?" I asked the officer.

"Sure," she smiled.

"Could you call Meryl for me?"

She looked down, shaking her head sadly. "I can't, I'm sorry Cristina."

"Please, I need her."

She closed her eyes tightly, I could see she wanted to help, she wanted to be able to just pick up the phone and tell her to come but I wasn't allowed any contact with her for a while.

"I need to tell her the truth, I need to tell everyone the truth."

She was getting closer to breaking I could see it in her face.

"I need to, I'll never see her again, I won't be able to live with myself if I don't get the chance to tell her the truth."

She looked around, "If Meryl says no, we say no more about it, if she comes and we get caught it's by coincidence, okay?"

I nodded.

"Good, stay here." She walked towards the double doors and disappeared into the rush of the hospital. I stayed alone waiting. What was I waiting for?

A doctor?

Meryl?

Dylan to come running back after me?

I kept my eyes on the door in case she came back. My hand didn't hurt so much anymore whether it's because I've gotten used to it or because of the overwhelming anticipation.

She was gone for a lot less time than I thought she'd be, surely with a phone call that quick she's rejected me. I didn't want to know if her answer was no, I couldn't live with the guilt and embarrassment of her rejecting me, I couldn't. I'd rather forget I even considered asking in the first place.

"She's on her way." She smiled; I couldn't contain my excitement. Meryl had agreed to see me, she agreed even after what I'd done. She's coming to see me. I smiled down at the floor.

"She's coming to see me," I whispered.

"She is," the officer said. She put her arm around me in a side hug. Tears began to form in my eyes, I couldn't tell if it was because she was crushing my hand or because I haven't had a hug in so long, I was beginning to forget how it felt.

"Cristina?" A woman dressed in blue scrubs called.

Finally

"Loving this fashion moment but could you put this on for me please." She said looking me up and down.

"Okay," I looked at the gown and then down at my hand, how I was going to get these jeans off without my hand was beyond me. "How?"

"I'll help you," the officer laughed.

SPARKS OF BETRAYAL

"Thanks, you're a star." I tilted my head back with a smile. I changed into the gown and began the walk down to the x-ray room.

"What made you punch the wall then?" The nurse asked, she was trying her best to make conversation.

"Men."

"Cristina, don't you hurt yourself over a man." She said, "my best friend Steph used to say, men aren't important. I live by that." She laughed.

"Don't you have a husband or anything?"

"How dare you assume I was straight." Her laugh was infectious, a mid-pitch chuckle. Her smile was stunning, her bright white teeth sparkled in the lights. I was mesmerized, but she wasn't as beautiful as Meryl. I wanted Meryl back.

I went into the x-ray room and let her do whatever she was doing. I tried to ignore the pain as much as possible and focused on the fact that Meryl was on her way to see me. She decided herself to go out of her way to see me even though she knows what I've done.

Or didn't do.

She was probably here by now and all I had to do to see her was get through this x-ray. I had to think carefully about how I was going to approach the situation. I had this opportunity to make things right I can't mess it up again. It was my last chance before I lost her forever, and I need her. I love her. I just hope she still loves me too.

"All done." The nurse smiled, "you can go to room seven down that corridor, I'll be there in a minute."

"Okay," I walked away my hand still clutching the other. I walked down the corridor to find room seven, I could see her through the window. Her beautiful hair rested on her shoulders, and the scars on her face were stunning. She wasn't smiling, I wasn't expecting her to. Her melancholy expression reminded me of autumn.

What was I supposed to say?

I took a deep breath before pushing through the door.

"Hi, Meryl." I said. My smile faded as I realized, she wouldn't look at me, she didn't say a word. She wasn't here because she loved me anymore it was because she wanted the truth. That hurt more than anything.

She didn't love me anymore.

People always used to tell me that as soon as I found the right person, I had to keep them close, look after them, and do everything to make them never want to leave. I failed; I'm here having done the complete opposite. I'm staring at the only person I've ever truly loved, the only person I can see myself spending the rest of forever with, the only person I would be happy with, but she doesn't feel nearly the same.

She hates me.

She doesn't want to see me.

She's only here for herself.

The most frustrating thing is that I have absolutely no right to be angry with her. No right to be upset. It's all my fault. She deserves someone better than me, she deserves the world.

"Meryl I-"

"How could you?" She interrupted, "why didn't you tell me?"

"I-"

"I'm sorry." She whispered.

"You don't have to apologize; you deserve the truth."

Chapter 3

It was Dylan, it was all his idea. No one would get hurt he said. Ben Matthews had been at work I could have sworn I saw him in the morning, so I sent the signal to Dylan. He put a lit match through the letter box, he must have placed it on the carpet because had he thrown it surely the match would have gone out. By the time I got there the house was up in flames, Dylan had been going round people telling them not to call for help because it had already been arranged, he didn't want to overwhelm the dispatchers he said, but he hadn't called anyone. He wanted to see the whole thing burn and he did. I was the one to finally call for help, I didn't tell them what had happened, just that there was a fire.

By the time they arrived, it was too late, the house was just a pile of ash. They couldn't get hold of Ben; it was only then that I realized he wasn't at work.

"Dylan!" I shouted, he came close enough for me to whisper, "they can't find Ben, did you check he wasn't inside?"

"I assumed he was at work." My heart sank to my stomach, not only had he watched the house burn he had left him inside to die.

"You're a monster, I'll make sure everyone knows what you've done."

He laughed, "All I need to do is match your DNA to a piece of evidence and you go down for life." He held up a small bag of burned things, a photo of my fingerprint and a strand of my hair.

"What the fuck Dylan?"

"You will do everything I ask of you. Everything."

What was I supposed to do?

"Tell someone." Meryl said. "You should have told them."

"Maybe I should have."

"That's not why I'm here." She sighed, "why has my house turned to ash? Why is my skin covered in scars? Why is Dylan walking free?"

I was still linked to his agreement, I basically belonged to him.

"He didn't tell me who's house we were at; I hadn't realised you'd moved." I pleaded, "I promise you I never would have helped him if I knew it was your house."

"But you would have if it was someone else's house?"

I could tell she wasn't here to forgive me. She was only here for closure, I had to accept that she wasn't going to fall for anything, there was no sympathy to come from her.

"I didn't say that, I would never hurt you."

"But you did."

"I didn't know that's what we were doing, I didn't know anything."

All I did was put the wooden box through the second-floor window, I had climbed the tree next to the house and thrown it inside. I didn't know what was inside, he told me not to ask, he told me to be quick, to not leave it too long. I assumed it was drugs or something, if I knew I wouldn't have done it. Not after what happened to Ben.

"I want to believe you, I really do."

SPARKS OF BETRAYAL

"Why don't you?" I asked, my voice had reduced to just more than whisper.

"I just don't understand why you never told me before."

"I'm sorry, you were reopening the case and I just felt like it gave you something to do while you were in hospital but as soon as you started putting the two cases together, I started getting scared." My eyes widened, by this point I was begging, begging her to see what he had done, begging her to see who I was. I'm not a monster.

"Scared I would find out?" She scoffed; I knew how stupid it sounded considering I had just told her everything.

"Scared that you'd hate me, that you'd decide that I'd done it and let it be. I was scared to lose you."

"You wouldn't have if you had just told me, explained before getting dragged away by the police, how was I supposed to feel?" Those words hurt me the most. Hearing her tell me that telling her the truth would have sorted everything out felt like I had betrayed myself.

"I'm sorry I didn't know anything about it. I suppose I thought I was out of the woods; I was ready to start the rest of forever with you."

"You understand how that's worse right?"

I tilted my head in confusion. "You we're never going to tell me because you thought you'd gotten away with it."

She looked disappointed in me; I didn't know what to say everything I did say seemed to be wrong. I was trying so hard for forgiveness, but I hadn't thought of how to do it. She shook her head in disbelief, she had the right to be annoyed at me and there was no way to force her into forgiving me, but I couldn't lose her. I already had; she was walking towards the door. I tried to stop her, but she was gone. I was alone again, forever. She wasn't ever coming back.

I stepped back falling onto the bed. I couldn't hold it in anymore. I had just lost the only thing I've ever cared about. Tears streamed down my face as I gasped for breath. My heart ached and the butterflies in my stomach turned to knots, my whole body shook with anger. I wasn't only angry at myself but Dylan too, none of this would have happened if he had just left me alone.

***

I returned to my flat, and Meryl still hadn't moved her things. I assumed she was going to be gone by the time I got back. I sat on my sofa in shock. I had gotten away with the murder charge, they let me go. It didn't mean I was innocent because technically I wasn't but maybe Meryl will consider staying with me. I sighed; I couldn't believe how desperate I was sounding; it was borderline

SPARKS OF BETRAYAL

childish. I shook my head and continued with the day. My hand was wrapped tightly to minimize swelling, but I'd walked away with nothing more than a bad bruise.

I didn't know what to do with myself, I wasn't supposed to be here. I was supposed to be locked up, far away from normal life, instead, I was sitting on the same sofa I've sat on for years, the same room I've lived in for as long as I can remember, even the food in the fridge is the same as I left it. I didn't think I'd ever see the black and white marble counter again or the dark grey cupboard doors. I never thought I would miss the shiny white walls or the plain black fridge or the oven, but I was grateful to still be here. Even the smell of my perfume still lingered in the air.

The door swung open violently Meryl skipped through joyfully. I stood up sharply. Our eyes met and she stopped, her smile faded, and her eyes narrowed. My heart got louder; I didn't know how she would react to me being back so soon. She ran up to me and embraced me in a hug. I was confused but I hugged her tightly I couldn't lose her again.

"What's going on?" I asked, shattering the silence.

"I got you out." She dug her head into my shoulder.

"You did?"

JUPITER

She nodded. "It wasn't you; it was Dylan. You did nothing wrong."

If I were her, I'd have never forgiven me, especially not so soon. She finally stepped away from me, she shuffled to the fridge and took out some leftovers. I stood in amazement.

Had she forgiven me?

Surely not.

"Do you want any?" She shouted as she started dishing some out onto her plate.

"Sure," I laughed. I was struggling to believe that I was home, with Meryl.

"Here you go," she gleamed handing me the plate. "I haven't completely forgiven you, but I appreciate that you didn't know what was happening."

I nodded, "Thank you." I didn't expect myself to whisper but something stopped my voice escaping.

She smiled at me. "Life's too short to make enemies."

Chapter 4

Midnight struck as I stepped into my room. I looked around at my things, they were exactly how I had left them. Of course, they were I was gone less than twenty-four hours, but I had imagined Meryl ripping everything, throwing it, destroying everything. She didn't, she left everything. That's the difference between her and me. I would have destroyed every single thing she owned, everything. Sure, I'd feel shit about it later, but I would have needed her to understand how I felt.

"Cristina?" Meryl said slowly stepping into the room. "Can I have some help?"

JUPITER

"Sure, what with?"

She lifted her joggers up to reveal her burns still hadn't healed. "Would you cover them?"

I nodded, making my way to the medical cupboard in the bathroom. I had spare bandages and things from before I grbbed the box and went back to my room.

"Bed or chair?" I pointed at the options as she looked around.

"Could I stand, they sting against both."

"I don't see why not." I said as I cleaned the burns. She was clearly in pain, so I was as gentle as possible.

"When was the last time you had these checked?"

"Two days ago."

"Okay." I thought for a second, I didn't know too much about burns, most of hers had healed and scarred, the second-degree ones but the few third-degree ones left on her legs were taking a while longer. I had to get her out of that hospital she had clearly had enough of being there I couldn't bear to see her so unhappy. Perhaps I should have left her there a while longer where she was with professionals, Steph was the one to send her home though but maybe just because she trusted me to know what I was doing.

SPARKS OF BETRAYAL

I finished covering the burns and stood up, we just stared at each other for a few seconds. Her beautiful dark eyes were locked with mine, i wanted to kiss her, I really did but the fear of rejection was too great for me to commit. We held eye contact for a few seconds longer before she stepped away.

"Goodnight, Meryl." She smiled as she left.

"Goodnight." I whispered back.

I got into bed and spent hours just staring at the ceiling until I finally fell asleep.

Chapter 5

" Listen, I was thinking about yesterday and wanted to know whether you would like to go out for lunch with me?" I smiled.

"I think you should keep a low profile for now, and make sure the police don't see you for a couple of days."

"What exactly did you do to get me out?"

"That's for me to know, I promise it'll all work out in the end." Her smile faded into to anger, "I'm getting my own back."

"You're what?" I choked, "Meryl, what have you done?"

SPARKS OF BETRAYAL

"Don't worry, I know people, and I know how to take Dylan down." She was staring up at the clock, it was nine in the morning, but it had been for months. "Every time I look at that clock it's 9 o clock." She laughed.

"I took the batteries out for my light in the bedroom and never replaced them."

She laughed, "and there's me thinking I'm some kind of wizard." Her laugh was my favourite sound, I loved her childish giggle, she hated it, tried to change it for years but it kept coming back. I think it's perfect.

"What people? Is it dangerous?" I questioned, reverting the conversation back.

"Not at all, they're old friends."

"Detective friends?"

She nodded; I wasn't completely convinced but I trusted her. She wouldn't do anything too stupid considering how much she'd seen over the years.

"Think what you're doing for a second Meryl, what do you want the outcome to be?"

"I want Dylan to pay. For what he did to me but mostly what he did to you."

"What?"

"Dylan needs to be locked up."

"No what do you mean he needs to pay for what he did to me? What about you Meryl, your house, your skin, your mental health... I think it's fair to say he's done more to you than to me."

"Either way, he's hurt us both. We can take him down together if you like?"

I nodded without thinking, not because I wanted to be a part of it. I didn't want anything to do with him but if it meant I was going to stop Meryl getting hurt by him again I would do anything.

Anything.

"I've got to be at the station for ten, you can come if you like."

"Didn't you literally say I needed to stay clear of police for a few days?"

"I'll sort it."

If Meryl said that she would sort it, she would. Every time. It's like she has some kind of ridiculous authority over everyone, they just listened and did what she told them to do.

"We better go then, we're late."

"What do you mean?"

"It's ten past." I laughed.

SPARKS OF BETRAYAL

"Shit, let me grab my jacket."

I opened the door and held it until she was through. I locked it and started walking down the stairs.

We reached the bottom and the fresh air hit us as the double door swung open. We walked faster and faster with each step toward the police station and as we finally arrived, we saw him. He was right in the window, couldn't miss him, couldn't mistake him, it was him.

"He's in there," I breathed, half out of breath from the speed walking, I hadn't walked that fast in years and half from panic, what would he do if he saw us here?

"I know, just don't make eye contact you'll be fine." She grabbed my hand; her skin was rough but comforting. She pulled me into the door, I felt nervous but excited to see what was going to happen.

Everyone watched us as we made our way into the back room.

"SHE'S IN HERE." Meryl screamed. I saw her light a match, this wasn't to get revenge on Dylan it was to get revenge on me. She ran away expecting the match to catch onto something, it didn't so I stepped on it putting the fire out. There was no way out, there were already officers coming towards me.

She lied to me.

JUPITER

She lied to me.

She lied to me.

I was dragged out into a police van that was ready outside.

"Meryl told me to give you this." The officer handed me a note, handwritten by Meryl.

Cristina,

I'm sorry, well I suppose I'm not really. I thought I could love you but now I know that I should have walked away when I had the chance. I suppose I should take this as a lesson in not trusting people, I spent my whole career trusting no one and as soon as I opened the door you stepped inside but I should never have let you in. Maybe that doesn't make sense to you but simply, I wish we had never met. I regret joining cadets, and I regret becoming a detective, those are words I never thought I'd say, I was born to solve crimes, but you ruined it for me.

SPARKS OF BETRAYAL

I loved you and you destroyed me. I could tell you were lying the second you opened your mouth about Dylan, that's why I was acting nice, I wanted to hold on to the final moments of love we had. I did it all because I had no choice, I couldn't trust you not to hurt me again. I'm only sorry for loving you, I'm sorry for caring about you. I've learnt my lesson.

This is the end. Sparks flew but they were nothing but Sparks of Betrayal.

Goodbye Cristina.

Meryl.

The End

Printed in Great Britain
by Amazon